BLOOD TEAR

LAZERIC LIPSCOMB

AuthorHouse™
1663 Liberty Drive
Bloomington, IN 47403
www.authorhouse.com
Phone: 1-800-839-8640

© 2010 Lazeric Lipscomb. All rights reserved.
No part of this book may be reproduced, stored in a retrieval system, or transmitted by any means without the written permission of the author.
First published by AuthorHouse   7/1/2010

Printed in the United States of America
Bloomington, Indiana
This book is printed on acid-free paper.

ISBN: 978-1-4520-2196-6 (e)
ISBN: 978-1-4520-2195-9 (sc)

Library of Congress Control Number: 2010907179

I would like to thank God because without him nothing is possible. I would like to thank my mother Elonda Lipscomb and my father Anthony Herron second because without them I wouldn't be possible. Next are the men that helped my mother raise me. Raymond, Antwaun and Rodney. I love ya'll, ya'll helped me become who I am.

To Lazeric jr., Avina, Adriana, and Andreya. My beautiful kids, I love ya'll, ya'll are my motivation. All of my nephews and nieces: Ray jr., Twaun jr., Rodney jr. Mainski, K'wan Re Re, Pebbles, Meek Meek, and all the rest of ya'll.

To my little brother Casius and my beautiful baby sister Ronique.

My grandparents Fannie and Herman Lipscomb. I love and thank ya'll for ya'll love and support. My uncles and aunties, Junior, ICE Rob, Cindy, Gina, Venus, Tricec, Linda and Sherry, Bootsy.

Grandma Sharon, Rusty, Grandpa Joe and my POPs Big RAY. POPs I'm not gone let you down I got you, just be easy.

My cousins, it's so many of ya'll so if I forget you don't be mad at me. India you my girl you were there when I really needed you. Wendy, Della, Tina, and Gina. Lil Herman, Jameca, Nicole, and Chey. Jerold, Darryl, Rita, KEVIN AKA YOUNG BOSS, I love you lil cuz. Rochell, Aaliyah, Ebony, Tia, Mariah, Marquise. I love all of ya'll and to all of my other cousins I love all of ya'll to.

The real VAIL street RANGERS and the VILL RANGERS and the real street niggas that I fuck with. Meechie, JJ, Steve, Ty skill, AP, JuJu, Byron, De De, Miz, B-Dolla, Toolie, 4 Meechie, 80 Proof, I ain't forgot about you, Von you too, Richard Gee, Richard L(Snagga Swagga), Man(2Low cousin), G Ray, G Stone, D BO, My brother Andre out in NY. Twanmoe, Lil Nate, Moose moe, 4 JJ, LIL Rick, Mal, Lil Marcus, 2Low Shakey, Jamel, BD, Popcorn, Nick bean, Tatta moe, Reese, and Mego, Donta C, Lil Stone, Baby Stone, The Brothers from Winchester.

To the other real niggas that I got live for and everybody that read my book before I put it out there, Rufus(the G) Brother J, 4 Lou, Lil Taker, LIL Bobby, Ren, K- Rag, (Kendall), Lil C (snoop), Big Food, Tone, Lil Carl, T- Bone(Buck Town) T-Bone(the G), A1, Van, LIL P(from Duck Town), Star, 4 Rell, Mose, lilG (TVL), Blood, M- Easy, Dub, Lil Charls, Butter, BUB, KeKe, KO 4, Ralph, Breed Slick, Breed Slim, Breed Lil ED, Sircon, Ken, Ace Boogie, Manny, 4 LilD, Allen- Tell Peaches I love her, BD slick,

E-moe, Mafia (big boy), Boobie, Bald head, Nine Nine, Tray G, Tone Bone, JB, RED- I aint 4got about you, True(ATL), Roop G, Black (the G), lil Moe Bubbles, Lil Timmy(Crank Town), LIL Mike(LK), Mr. 773(cello), Bowlegs, Lil D(GD), 2X, BIG G,DA PRINCE JUNE BUG, JL, PUSHA, Pitt, LIL Breed(DP),LIL JOE, G-Meechie, Deandre, And Mississippi.

To PLAYBOY THE BEAR and the ZOOCREW and MAYNE C, I LOVE YA"LL

To my Twins mother SABRINA you MRS. BEAST so ima Always love you.

To Amanda thank you for my first two kids.

To Sadiyah,Kaira,Tina, Rozena, Quita, Domo, Nish Rella , Tarra, April, Toya Barnes, Nikkie ,Maurice Roper, Bubbles, Aisha, Anja, Avis, Brittany, Eric L, CO CO, Patty, Kitty, KITA, Ebony, Diana, Biggie, Gay, Tasha, Donald, Everybody in the trap on the last block.

To my sun Duggy, I love you bruh. And I call you Sun cause you shine like one. I thank you bruh because you motivated me to keep going with this book. You believed in me before I believed in myself. I owe you.

To Ma Ma and Sherry, I love ya'll, ya'll are my beautiful daughters.

R.I.P LIL B, LIL Brandon, LIL G, and Cee Cee. Ya'll will forever be missed.

HOUSTON YOU THE MAN.

IF I FORGOT ANYBODY PLEASE FORGIVE ME BUT LET ME KNOW.

TO GRAND MONEY AND ALL OF THE GMG'S OUT THERE…

 TO COACH TYSON BECAUSE HE ALWAYS TOLD ME "FINISH STRONG SON".

BLOOD TEAR

CHAPTER 1

"Ay C.O., on that H-well." The guy's in the day room hollered as they heard someone pounding on the H-well door. The C.O. woke up out of his sleep, but remained seated until he heard the pounding. When he got up and pressed the button to open the door, Lil J walked through it.

"I beat that shit jo! I'm outta this bitch!" Lil J hollered as the door closed behind him.

"Damn, you beat that shit?" One of the guys that walked up to the gate asked.

"Hell yeah I beat it. NOT GUILTY! NOT MUTHA FUCKIN' GUILTY!"

"Give me yo I.D. and go on the deck." The C.O. said as he pressed another button.

Lil J gave the C.O. his I.D. card and pulled the gate open. As he walked through it, the guys in the day room flooded him with questions about what happen in court.

"You say that they found you not guilty right? What happened tho?" One of the guys that was fighting a case similar to his asked, wanting to get kind of an idea of how things would go if he ever made it that far. But unfortunately for him, Lil J wouldn't be able to provide him with the information that he was looking for because his trial only lasted for five hours.

"Ain't shit happen really because they ain't have enough evidence." Lil J said as he laid his paper work down on the table.

"What happened with the witnesses? What they was saying?"

"Them bitches ain't even show up."

"Ay Leebo." the C.O. called out. "What up?"

"You know the side you on locked down right?" the C.O. said referring to the half and half that the county was doing due to the 18 and 6 lock down. "I'ma let you stay out until they call for you tho', aight?"

"That's cool." Lil J said before he walked over to a guy named Chris that was on the phone. "Ay who got the phone after you?"

"What?" Chris asked a little vexed that his phone call was being interrupted.

"Who after you on the phone?"

"Block Burner, but I don't think he gone trip if you go before him since you just came back from court."

"Aight, let me see it after you then."

"I got you." Chris said before he went back to his phone conversation.

While Lil J was sitting back waiting for the phone, he thought back to the night that brought him to where he was now. It was the middle of September back in 2005.

Lil J was out in the projects in Robbins leaving out of a broad name Laquita's crib, and when he approached the parking lot he saw about six niggas all up on his car. He knew that he was gonna have some problems out of the niggas sooner or later from the despising looks that they gave him every time he came through their hood in different whips. He was just waiting for the day when he would come out of Laquita's crib and find his car gone or his rims missing so that he could come back with his goons and chop they shit up.

But now that the niggas was disrespecting him by being all up on his whip. He felt that the time had come, and wanted to pull out the 30 shot 9mm that was in his back pocket, and give the niggas the business; but he was out numbered, and probably out gunned too, and he knew that if he pulled a stunt before he got in his whip his chances of making it out of the projects alive would be slim to none. So as he approached his car he spoke.

"Aye won't ya'll get off my whip."

"Nigga fuck you, and this pussy ass whip, we a take this bitch." One of the guys that was known as Lil Pete snapped.

"Yo clown ass gone stop coming through here stunting like you the shit, or like shit sweet over here." B-low, one of the guys that was sitting on the car said before him and his guys started moving away from it.

B-low and his guy's knew that Lil J was from Harvey and wanted to hit him, but the only thing that was stopping them was that they didn't know if he was connected or not, and didn't want to bring another unnecessary war to their hood if he was.

While the guys was talking shit and sending threats, Lil J bit down on his bottom lip still fighting the urge, and played it cool. He always pulled in backwards when he parked, and his windows was tinted so when he got in the car and started it up, the guys couldn't see what he was doing until he hopped back out with a Mac'11 that he had pulled out of his stash, spot and let it ride; fatally wounding Lil Pete, B-low, and another one of the guys that was leaning on his car before he jumped back in his whip, and sped off. By the time the guy's finally upped their guns and started letting off shots, it was too late because the Charger that Lil J was in was already fish tailing around the corner, and out of the projects.

"Ay Leebo. John Leebo." the C.O. said bringing Lil J back to the present.

"I'm right here, what's up?"

"Go pack yo shit, they just called for you."

"Pop cell 17."

"I already popped it, just hurry up."

"Aight." Lil J said before he grabbed his paperwork and walked off.

Lil J had a light brown skin complexion, and a handsome face with 360's in his head that was spinning out of control. Some considered him to be a cox-comb from the way that he stayed in the mirror brushing his hair all day. He wasn't a sociable person before he came to jail, but being in the county for almost two years forced him to acclimatize.

Earlier in the day Lil J had beat his case in trial. He had been locked up for almost two years with no bond for a triple murder. The evidence that the State had against him wasn't enough for the Judge to find him guilty on the charges, especially when the witnesses didn't show up. So hearing the Judge say "not guilty" was the best thing that Lil J had heard in the twenty-one months that he had been locked up. His lawyers tried to get him a bond three times, but each time the State found ways to convince the Judge that he was dangerous to the community, and a possible flight risk. So he didn't have any other choice but to sit in the county jail on 26th and California, in Division One for twenty-one months waiting for this day.

His guys stayed in his corner, but some of his bitches broke bad. He really didn't trust hoes anyway, so he wasn't tripping. He looked at them like a pawn in a chess game, they were all expendable.

While Lil J was packing his things, the guys that was out of their cells was all in his cell trying to get him to leave them something. He had acquired a lot of valuable things in the twenty-one months that he'd been locked up; things that couldn't be bought on commissary, like du rags, wave brushes, wife beaters, and a lot of other things that held value in jail. He even had some weed and "X" pills that he was getting in through one of the female C.O.'s that he was messing with.

"What up Lil J? Hit me with something man." was all Lil J kept hearing while he was packing.

"I ain't try'na fuck with that shit man, all I wanna do is get my pictures, and my mail so I can get the fuck out of here."

"Come on Lil J get off that bullshit." the guy with the similar case hollered.

Lil J stopped packing and looked around the cell to see what he could give the guys. Him and his celly's commissary boxes was filled with commissary, and they had about eight brown grocery bags under their bunks that was also filled with commissary. He had already gave his celly the weed and the "X" pills, so he just grabbed two of the brown bags from under his bunk.

"Here, ya'll can split this shit."

"That's love!" the guys hollered as they dipped off to go split the commissary.

"Ay Lil J, don't forget to hit us man," the guys that was locked in their cells hollered onto the catwalk.

"Aight I got ya'll don't trip. I'ma leave it with my celly. Ay Blue hit them niggas for me, and hit 'em right man don't play them." Lil J said to his celly knowing damn well that he was gone play them anyway.

"I'ma hit them cats right. You just gone and get up out of here."

"Aight I'm up Blue, just hit that number I gave you." Lil J said before he grabbed his mail and pictures along with the bed roll that he had to turn in and walked out of the cell and up towards the gate. "Aight my niggas, I'm up." Was the last words that Lil J said before leaving the deck.

ಲ

"Unh..uh..Unh." Tameka moaned, as Cash pounded her out from the back. He had her bent over the arm of her living room couch with her skirt pulled up over her voluptuous ass and her thong pulled to the side, while his pants was pulled down to just above his knees. "Unh..unh..ooh shit... ooh..I'm cummin." Tameka exclaimed as her phone started ringing for the second time. "Unh..unh..Cash wait! let me get...let me see who that is."

Tameka was known in the hood as one of Lil J's main pieces before he went to jail. She was a Puerto Rican and Black beauty that was standing 5' 6" with some long sandy brown hair that hung to the middle of her back, and some 36C's that stood firm. But what was really killing everything hands down, and gave her the "Baby Got Back Award", was how far her round plumped ass stuck out.

"Hell nah....fuck that phone." Cash said in between strokes, as he began pounding harder.

Cash was a laid back playa that got money and stayed to his self, unless he was with a broad or in the middle of a dice game; which he always was.

He was a brown skin somewhat slim cat with braids, and had some green eyes that drove all of the ladies crazy. He made a living by selling weed and breaking dice games, and although he never went around asking for trouble, he never ducked it when it came his way.

"Unh..Unh...yeah..ooh shit yeah." Tameka moaned, loving the pounding that she was receiving.

"Ah fuck..Ahhhh." Cash hollered as he pulled his self as deep as he could inside Tameka before releasing his load inside of her.

Tameka had already came and was still enjoying the feeling until her phone started ringing for the third time. "Damn, who the hell is that?" she asked herself as Cash pulled out of her and walked towards the bathroom.

"Gone 'head and answer it, cause whoever it is, they thirsty as hell." said Cash.

"Shit, this ain't nobody but my friend Aliana. I wonder what the hell she blowing my phone up for." Tameka said before answering the phone. "Girl why you blowing me up?"

"Because I have something to tell you, and you ain't gone believe what it is."

Tameka started thinking to herself about what could've been so unbelievable that Aliana had to tell her. She thought long and hard, and only came up with Lil J and the amount of time that he had probably got.

She was suppose to had went to court and watched his trial earlier that day, but when Aliana came to pick her up, she was still sleeping and didn't feel like getting up, so she told Aliana that she wasn't going.

She felt like Lil J didn't have a chance in hell at beating his case anyway, knowing that the State had two eyewitnesses against him. So she really didn't see the point in going to court just to see him get convicted.

"Meka!" Aliana hollered bringing Tameka back from her thoughts.

"What?"

"Did you hear what I said?"

"Yeah, and I ain't got time for guessing games, so tell me what it is." Tameka said as she walked into the bathroom as Cash was coming out.

Aliana knew that Tameka didn't think Lil J was coming home from the numerous conversations that they had about him. Tameka used to always talk about how much she missed and loved Lil J, but Aliana knew that she was lying because after every conversation, she would always say that he was never coming home because of the eyewitnesses that was against him.

Aliana loved her friend, but what she didn't like about her was how she said "Forget

Lil J." and left him for dead when he got locked up.

It wasn't like he didn't take care of her when he was out, because he did that and some. He gave her everything she wanted and put her up in her own apartment. So Aliana didn't understand why she played him the way she played him.

But now that he was coming home and Tameka didn't know anything about it. Aliana wanted to see how she would react once she heard the news.

"Lil J beat his case today!" Aliana screamed into the phone.

Tameka's blood ran cold as she froze trying to comprehend what she had just heard. She knew that her friend had to be playing because what she just heard couldn't be true.

"Yeah right girl. I already knew that he was gone get found guilty, so you ain't gotta lie to me. But anyway, how much time did he get?" Tameka asked as she pulled off her thong and began wiping herself after soaping up a towel.

"Girl he ain't get found guilty, so he ain't get no time. As a matter of fact, he should be on his way home right now."

Tameka didn't respond, she just started laughing.

"What the hell is so funny?"

"Ali, be for real. Lil J had two eye witnesses against him that say they saw him shoot them boys, now do you really expect me to believe this bullshit you telling me? Girl stop it with the shenanigans." Tameka said, hoping that Aliana was playing because she just couldn't bear the thought of Lil J getting out treating her like shit; which she knew he would from the way that she treated him while he was in.

"Meka I wouldn't play about no shit like this. That nigga beat that shit. I heard the judge say not guilty my damn self."

Tameka became enraged. "So you still went to watch his trial even though I told you I wasn't going?"

"Hell yeah I went. I sho' didn't get up early for nothing. But look, I'm on my break so ima call you back later bye." Aliana said hanging up before the conversation went somewhere where they both didn't need it to go.

Tameka took the phone away from her ear and looked at it.

I know the fuck this bitch didn't just hang up on me. I'ma have to check-.

"What was that all about?" Cash asked, interrupting Tameka's thoughts. He was on his way to let her know that he was about to leave until he heard her say something about somebody getting found guilty and getting some time. And the only person that she messed with that was locked up was Lil J.

"That wasn't shit. My friend ass tripping on some bullshit."

"Who was she talking about, Lil J?"

"Yeah, she talking about he beat his case earlier, and should be on his way home right now."

"He beat his case?" Cash asked, getting real apprehensive.

"Naw, I told you she was tripping."

"And how the hell you figure that?"

"Because he had two eyewitnesses against him. "And why you worried about if he beat his case or not? What you scared of him or something?

"Hell naw I ain't scared, but I ain't stupid either. I done saw too many niggas get crossed out over dog hoes." Cash said as he turned around and walked off.

"Dog hoes! Nigga you better watch how the fuck you talk to me!" Tameka said to Cash who was already on his way out the door.

Cash knew better then to stick around if Lil J was really on his way home. He didn't want to get caught up in any domestic disputes that didn't have nothing to do with him, and Tameka was just a fuck to him anyway. He couldn't see hisself messing around with her because she wasn't loyal.

"Fuck you Cash. You is scared of him. Gone head and take yo punk ass back to that ugly bitch of yours." Tameka said before she slammed the door.

Fuck that nigga! He can't fuck anyway, she thought to herself as she picked up the phone to make a few calls to see if Lil J was really coming home.

☙

When Lil J walked out of Division Five, he couldn't help but to smile as the June heat embraced him. When he got popped by the law, he came into the county jail rocking a Evisu fit, some Air Force Ones and a Sean Jean leather, but due to the fact that the guys down in the storage room be stealing clothes when niggas come in with new gear, he had to leave out rocking a white T, two pairs of boxers, a pair of socks, and some shower shoes.

The guards tried to get him to wear some clothes out of the poor box, but he wasn't going. He told them that he would rather leave out naked then to put somebody else's clothes on. So as he walked through the gate, his guys X and Mikey fell out laughing while his right hand man Zed just looked on bemused.

"Damn man, where the fuck yo clothes at? Don't tell me that you done let some nigga take yo shit?" Mikey inquired.

Mikey was tall and slim with a high yellow skin complexion. He was the youngest out of Lil J's crew, and although he wasn't a bad looking guy, he wasn't considered handsome either.

"Come on now, you know if that was the case I'll still be up in there fighting a jail house murder. A nigga ain't taking shit from me but some hot slugs or an ass whuppin. But nah, ya'll know how them thirsty ass cats be up in the storage room. As soon as some hot shit come through they get to stealing, and it just so happens that my shit came up missing and don't nobody know shit."

"I see you done got a lil bigger up in there."

"Shit what you expect; ain't nothing else to do in there but eat and work out. I woulda been bigger than this if they woulda had some free weights up in that bitch."

"So what's up?" X asked.

X was one of Lil J's laid back goons. He wasn't tall nor was he considered short, but standing at 5' 10" and weighing 200 pounds, he made it known that he was far from a shorty.

He was laid back most of the time, but when shit got crazy he made sure that his presence was known.

"You already know what's up, take me back to the hood nigga." Lil J responded.

"Ay, whatever happened to them lames that stabbed you the fuck up in there?"

"Them bitch ass niggas was in Division Nine. I couldn't even get to 'em because them people wouldn't let me out the building; and I couldn't catch they ass at court like they got me. So I sent a kite over to one of my guys from 51st and Lowe. He was holding it down in nine around the time I got hit up, so when he got the kite he made them niggas feel it."

As they were approaching X's truck, Lil J stopped mid sentence as he noticed the truck for the first time. "This ain't never that new Lac truck with the vents on the side. And what these is, sixes on this bitch?" Lil J asked as he admired the exterior of the truck before opening the door. When he hopped in he saw that the interior was shutting shit down just like the exterior. X had leather everywhere and TV's was all through his shit. He had 8" monitors in the head rests, a 13" in the dash board, and a 17" flip in the center. " This bitch TV'd and leathered out huh? I see you done went and over did it." he said before his guys hopped in the truck behind him.

"Yeah I told you that you was gone have to get yo weight up when you came home." X said as he pulled off and headed for the E-way.

"So what's up J?" Zed asked as he spoke up for the first time since Lil J came out of Division Five.

"I just told y'all what's up. Take me back to the land nigga."

"Come on nigga, you know what the fuck I'm talking about. You know just like I know that when mu'fuckas get locked up and do a lil time, they get out on some, I'm done with the streets, I changed my life over type of shit. So tell me J, what's really good?"

Zed was Lil J's right hand man; and even though Lil J trusted all of his guys with his life. He knew that as long as Zed was by his side, he wouldn't have no problems that went unsolved. Zed was a dark skinned, well built playa with long jet black hair that he inherited from his Indian grandmother. He had a twin brother named Zep, and together they was a deadly combination.

"Yeah nigga, that's why I love yo mu'fuckin ass. You always on business and don't never sugar coat shit. But you know what? I ain't even gone stunt. I thought about that shit; about changing my life and leaving the streets alone. But then I thought about all of the real niggas that went to jail and changed they life and left the streets alone when they got out. I thought about how they let they guard down and thought that they was gone be safe just because they changed they life and found God, but the next thing they knew they was changed over paying God a visit. So you know what? Pass me my bitch, and fill me in on all of the shit that I need to know."

"My mutha fuckin nigga." said X.

"Fuck that old bitch. I got two new honey's right here for you. You know I keep the best shit." Zed said as he hit a few buttons and watched the door panel move to reveal a stash spot.

When Lil J saw Zed grab a text book size leather case from the stash spot and hand it to him he spoke up. "I see you put a stash spot in here too huh?"

"Yeah, I hooked this bitch up didn't I? I got that put in on Halsted at the Sounds and Rims shop. They got all type of shit up in there."

When Lil J opened the leather case he pulled out two gray and black twin .45 Rugers. "Damn jo, where you get these bitches from?"

"My out of town connect, I'll never mention his name I promise respect." Zed said as they all laughed.

"Ahhh come on with that bull shit. But anyway, what's up with my extended clips? You know how I get down."

"Yeah I know, but the gun shop out in Indiana said they only got fifteen shot clips for them, and I ain't been out to the one in Riverdale yet."

"Aight so where the fifteen shot clips at then?"

"Be easy nigga, I got 'em at the spot with the rest of the guns and shit. Them clips that's in there right now is ten shots each. But forget all that, let me put you up on what's going on in the hood right now."

CHAPTER 2

The news about Lil J beating his case had spread through the streets before he was even released. Lil J and his guys was a problem to a lot of niggas in the hood. Him and his guys was known for getting money and better known for wilding; and for those two reasons, him and his guys had made a lot of enemies. That's also the reason why right now, on the other side of town, in a low key spot in Midlothian, three hitters was laid back strapped like book bags getting fucked up patiently waiting.

"Here Tray." Donta said as he passed Tray a blunt after he hit it a few times.

Donta was a dark skinned slim cat that couldn't have weighed no more than a hundred and forty pounds soaking wet, but he kept up enough shit to make niggas look at him like a behemoth. He was real humble when he wasn't scheming, but when it was time to get on business, all of that humble shit went out the window.

"Ay Donta?, how much longer do you wanna wait before we hit the streets and go get this bitch ass nigga? I mean shit, he should be out by now. What you think?" Tray asked before he hit the blunt.

Tray was just wild and didn't give a fuck. He stayed ready to rob any and every nigga that was getting it in, and out the hood. He was light skinned and short with a medium build, but what he used to his advantage was his boyish looks, because when he approached niggas that didn't know him they would see just an innocent little boy until they found their selves being robbed at gun point.

"What time is it?" Donta inquired.

Tray hit the blunt a few more times and exhaled the smoke before looking at his watch.

"Its eight forty five."

"We gone wait about another hour before we hit the streets. And we got all week to get this nigga so be cool."

"I think we should hit this nigga today while he ain't expecting it." Tray said as he hit the

blunt again before he passed it to Los. "You know he probably gone be partying and shit because he just came home. So I think this the perfect day to catch him slipping."

Donta grabbed his cup off the table and took a few sips of his Gray Goose. "You know what Tray? You right. Today is the perfect day, but not only because we can catch Lil J slipping, but because that nigga Rick said that he gone give us twenty Gs for killing Lil J. And remember I told ya'll that he gone give us an extra five for every one of his niggas that we take with him."

"Ay jo, I hope ya'll don't think taking Lil J and his niggas out gone be as easy as it sounds." Los said before he hit the blunt a few times and exhaled the smoke before putting the roach out. "I mean these niggas killas just like us. And as far as catching them niggas slipping, yeah today is the perfect day, but them twins gone be on point."

Los was black and Puerto Rican, so most looked at him as a pretty boy. He wasn't as treacherous as Donta or Tray but he made it known many a times that he wasn't to be fucked with. With his long wavy hair and athletic body, he could've had any bitch he wanted, but he chose to stay stuck on his baby mama.

"You talking about Zed and Zep?" Tray asked as he fired up another blunt.

"Yeah, I been watching how they get down, and from what I've seen, them niggas don't play no games."

"The fuck you doing watching them cats?" Donta inquired.

"Come on man, you know I watch every mu'fucka. I stay try'na find me a stain. I was try'na catch them niggas slipping a few months ago and rape they ass for everything they had."

"So what happen?"

"Like I said before, ain't no catching them slipping. So I just fell back because they be on point. Tray, you remember that night I called you and told you that I had a stain, then I called you right back and told you to forget about it?"

"You talking about back in March?"

"Yeah, them the mu'fuckas I was talking about hitting, but when I was following them all of a sudden my cell phone started ringing with a blocked number on the caller I.D. I let it ring tho' because I don't answer blocked calls or unknown numbers, but they called back like six times so I answered ready to snap, but the voice that came through the phone shook the fuck outta me. It was that nigga Zep. He told me about every time I followed them from start to finish, what cars I was in and all. When I asked him how he got my number, he ignored me and told me that if I didn't want shit to get real then I better fall back, then hung up. I thought about getting down on them niggas, but I didn't want something small to turn into something big, so I just fell back and said fuck 'em."

"Damn, you shoulda called me up, we coulda changed (killed) them bitches." said Donta.

"Nah man, it really wasn't shit so I said fuck it. But anyway, what the fuck Lil J do to Rick to make him put this hit on his head?"

"To tell you the truth, I don't fucking know, but I think it might have something to do with them bodies he just beat."

"Yeah it gotta have something to do with that shit," Tray said after he passed the blunt to Los. "Because from what I heard, that nigga Lil J was chilling with a bitch out in the projects in Robbins, and when he came out of her crib it was niggas sitting on his car straight up disrespecting his shit. When he told the niggas to get off his whip, a few of 'em started talking shit. They say Lil J played it cool until he got in his car, and the next thing they knew he upped a chopper and let that bitch holler. Three people got changed that night and one of them ended up being Rick's lil brother. So that gotta be the reason for the hit."

"Man I don't give a fuck why he want this nigga hit." said Donta . The only thing I give a fuck about is the money being right when this shit is over, but fuck all that, pass that mu'fucking weed.

☙

"Damn, so you telling me that this nigga Rick out there putting money on my head, and got mu'fuckas out there right now waiting to take me out?" Lil J inquired.

"Yeah, but that's only half the beef we gotta worry about. Them niggas from Robbins been coming through on bullshit ever since that shit happened out there. And Zep got word from a bitch that them stick up niggas from 146th and Loomis in on the hit that's on yo head." said Zed.

"You talking about Donta, Tray, and Los?"

"Yeah, Zep be fucking with Los baby mama and she told him that she didn't want him around you when you came home because she overheard Los talking to Tray and Donta about killing you and whoever with you."

"Damn this shit crazy. Look, the first thing we need to do is get rid of them stick up niggas. Then we gone go holler at Rick because I really don't want no trouble with dude, but I ain't ducking none. That nigga bleed just like I do. And as far as them niggas from Robbins, fuck them bitches, they the mu'fuckers that had me hit at court. I can't wait to go back out there and burn the rest of them bitches."

"I'm with you my nigga, but I don't know why you ain't just let us take care of them niggas while you was locked up, we coulda been burn them bitches." said X.

"Yeah I know, but I needed ya'll to lay low just in case something went wrong with my case, because if we all locked up who we gone have on the outside to take care of business for us?"

"You right , but what's up now?"

"Boy you see these two bitches right here?" Lil J said as he raised the two Rugers up in the air. "I'm ready to break these bitches in."

"Ay put them mu'fuckas down before you get us popped out here. You know how them people (police) like riding in unmarked cars on the E-way." said Mikey.

"Aight you right. I ain't try'na get popped out here for no dumb shit, but anyway what's going on with the block?"

"It's still doing a lil something. Things slowed up a lil bit on the weight. When that shit happened with them niggas in Robbins, and you got popped, Rick made Calvin raise the prices so we said fuck him and started copping from some cat named Jose from the Dark Side. The flavor that he got good, but it's just not as good as the shit Rick got."

"Ay tell him about the new spot we got on the nine." said X.

"Aw yeah, don't you remember them buildings on 159th on Lexington?"

"You talking about over there by the train tracks?"

"Yeah, we opened up a spot over there a few months ago and sent a few workers from the block over there. It was a few niggas over there that was try'na get a lil money, but they wasn't on shit so we hit'em and put'em down on our team."

"That's what's up, but that's some bitch ass shit that Rick pulled on them prices. We might have to change his ass sooner or later. I know he don't think we just gone sit back like some bitches while he sending hits and shit. And them mu'fuckas from Loomis already know how we get down so I don't know what the fuck they think they on."

"I got Zep and K.B watching them clowns right now because I know they might try to make a move on some slick shit." said Zed.

"Aight that's good shit, but where the hell Reggie at?"

"He in the hood holding the block down right now."

"Call him and tell him to grab a few of the shorties and set up some security. Let him know that we gone be there in ten minutes."

"Ay Lil J, you know Rick well connected right?" X inquired.

"Yeah I know all about him and his uncles, but what's that suppose to mean?"

"Nothing really, because I'm down with you till' the death, but you know if something happen to him, and niggas find out that we had something to do with it, we gone have more niggas try'na kill us than we can handle."

"I already know X, but I'm not about to just sit back and let him kill me. But you know what? These niggas at me not ya'll; so if any of ya'll wanna fall back that's cool with me. I mean ya'll ain't have shit to do with what happened."

"We been riding with you ever since we jumped in the game, so it'll be kinda crazy for us to turn our backs on you now. But anyway before we make a move on Rick, we gone do like you said and go holler at him first." said Zed.

"Yeah, Im'a try to get him to fall back because that shit that happened wasn't even my fault. Them niggas brought that shit on their selves."

"X, stop at the liquor store before we hit the block." said Mikey.

CHAPTER 3

"Come on Tank man I got you, just give me a little bit more time." A young man named Spankey pleaded as he laid on the ground banged up pretty bad from the beating that Tank was putting on him.

"Shut yo bitch ass up!" Tank hollered as he delivered a few more kicks to Spankey's face. "I gave yo bitch ass a little bit more time the last time, and you still ain't got my shit. I'm beginning to think that you little mutha fuckas around here starting to take me for a joke."

Tank was a real beast of a man that gave games not a chance. He was a pitch black, 6' 4", 250 pound solid animal with a mean mug that demanded respect. And although most niggas was intimidated by his size, it was his gangsta ways that really instilled fear in their hearts.

"Nah man, it ain't even like that. It's just that somebody stole my shit this time."

Spankey was a young cat that always seemed to find his self in fucked up situations with the wrong people. He was a good little dude, in fact, some could even consider him to be loyal. But he just seemed to lack in the field of getting money because he always found his self fucking it up. The last time that he came up short with Tank's money, he claimed that the police had popped the stash off, which they really did, so Tank gave him a pass and overlooked it, but this time Tank wasn't trying to hear that shit.

"Nigga how is it that everybody else around here can keep up with they shit , but when it comes down to you, yo shit keeps coming up missing?"

"I don't-"

"Ay give the lil nigga another pass man," Tone said cutting Spankey off. "At least he ain't ducking you like some of these other mutha fuckas a be doing if they was short with yo money."

Tone was Tank's little cousin on his mother side. One would have never knew that they were cousins unless they told you, because there was no resemblance save for their rebellious and treacherous ways. Tone was about three inches shorter than Tank with a light brown skinned complexion. He had braids and was a little on the chubby side, but he moved like a skinny nigga.

"You know this ain't the first time Shorty fucked up my money right?"

"Yeah I know, but we gotta go get up with Mack and Rob, so give Shorty a pass and lets ride."

" You lucky my man got sympathy for yo punk ass." Tank said as he kicked Spankey in the face again, this time breaking his nose. "Now hurry up and get out of here before I change my mind."

Spankey struggled to get to his feet then ran off holding his bloody face.

Tank was holding it down out in the old projects in Robbins, along with Tone, Mack, and Rob. They had about twenty to thirty young wild soldiers that was ready to ride whenever given the word. Back in 2005 when B-low, Lil Pete, and Von got changed, Tank and his guys went through shooting up Lil J's block for two months straight seeking revenge until Rick got them to calm down. He told them that he wanted Lil J dead just as bad as they did, but going through his block while he wasn't there was meaningless because they wasn't doing nothing but bringing unnecessary heat and attention to their selves, so Tank pulled his guy's back. But when he got word that Lil J beat his case, he sent Mack, Rob, and a few of his young soldiers out to Harvey.

CHAPTER 4

Lil J grew up in Chicago Heights living with his mother until the Department of Children's Family Services found out about her cocaine addiction. The department was already threatening to take Lil J away from her because of the numerous calls of neglect that they was receiving from the neighbors, so by her not wanting him to get caught up in the system, she sent him to Harvey to live with his father.

After about a week of living with his father, he realized that living with him wasn't going to be any different from living with his mother, because his father had a bad drinking problem.

At the age of thirteen, he felt like he was all alone because his father was always gone or too drunk to spend some real time with him, so he turned to the streets for guidance, soaking-up game from the dope fiends, and the prostitutes in the hood. He took heed to the game that the dope fiends dropped on him, but one particular dope fiend that he really respected was Slick, because Slick wasn't some old dirty scratching dope fiend that went around begging to support his habit. He usually had his own money when he came through to cop, but if he didn't, he would come through with his chrome .44 bull dog, and take what he wanted.

Slick had started taking a liking to Lil J from the way that he carried his self. When he looked at Lil J, he saw the same little avid thirteen year old that he used to be, and knew that he had the potential to become a beast if he had the right guidance, so Slick dropped some game on him every time he came around.

After Slick felt like he had dropped enough jewels on Lil J about the crack, and dope game, he went on the other side of town and robbed a lame that he knew was holding on the weight, then rode down on Lil J. "Ay lil' nigga, come take a ride wit' me real quick." Slick said in an authoritative tone of voice, as he pulled-up on him.

Lil J was in the middle of smoking a blunt, and telling his friends about a fifteen year old girl that he had did his thang with; and his friends was listening intently as the story was just about getting good before Slick interrupted him. "Aight here I come." Lil J said as he hit the blunt again before passing it to X. "I'ma get up wit' ya'll later if I don't come right back."

"Ay J you cool?" Zed asked, not liking the tone of voice that Slick used when he addressed Lil J.

"Yeah, I'm good Zed." Lil J said as he showed his guys some love before hopping in the car with Slick.

Slick couldn't help but to crack a smile as he saw how tight Lil J and his friends were. He also like the way that they looked after each other; but he had seen this type of love in the past amongst his so called "friends".

The love was all there, and it was genuine; at least it seemed that way, until niggas started cracking under pressure, and freezing up at the wrong time.

"What's good bruh?" Lil J asked, interrupting Slick's thoughts.

"Shit, you tell me. What's up wit' the weed?" Slick asked as he put the car in drive and pulled off.

"Aw shit, my bad. What you wanted to hit it?"

"Hell nah, you know I don't mess wit' nothing but the D."

"In that case then ain't nothin' up wit' it."

"You think smokin' that shit cool don't you?"

"Nah, not really." Lil J responded wondering what Slick was really tryna to get at.

"Then why you smokin' it then?"

"The same reason you snort dope, to get high."

"Aw what you try'na get smart now?"

"Nah, I'm just try'na figure out why you comin' at me like this."

"I'm coming at you like this because I know you too smart to be doing something so stupid."

"How is getting high considered to be doing something stupid?" Lil J asked with an addled look on his face.

"Tell me how you benefitting from it?"

Lil J thought about the question for a second before he responded – "I'm not."

"Exactly, and that's exactly the reason why I told you to try'da benefit from everything that you do, and to stay away from things that you ain't gaining from, because that's the only way that you gon' prosper in this cold and unfair world. But look, I ain't come pick you up to talk about this bullshit, and you gon' do whatever you want anyway, so I'm just gon' get down to the reason that I really came to pick you up." Slick said as he pulled over and parked his car in front of an apartment building that one of his broads named Boo Boo stayed in. "Do you remember the last time we hollered and you told me that you was tired of being broke?"

"Yeah, I remember."

"Well, if I told you that I had a way for you to make some money, would you be down?"

"Hell yeah I'll be down." Lil J replied with excitement in his voice.

Slick looked at Lil J and shook his head before he spoke.

"I think everything I tell you be going in one ear and out the other. What the hell I tell you about paying attention to what you getting' yoself into before you go jumping off the porch?"

"Aw yeah, I fa'got."

"Like hell you fa'got. Now come on and let's go up stairs for a minute."

Slick was a real OG from the Westside of Chicago who had came out to Harvey to lay low after eliminating a few niggas that him and his guys was beefing with. He had just came home from doing a stretch, and as soon as he got back to da hood, he found out that it was going down; so by him being the beast that he was, he jumped right down, and got it cracking.

When bodies started coming up missing, niggas started running and hiding because they feared Slick, and wanted him dead or off the streets. They knew that their chances of killing him was slim to none, so they did the only thing they could do, turn to the police.

When Slick and Lil J made it up to Boo Boo's apartment, Slick went into one of the back rooms while Lil J plopped down on the living room couch, and turned the TV on. Five minutes later, Slick entered the living room carrying a brown bag that contained 2 ½ ounces of crack, and 5 grams of dope.

"If you down, and still wanna get money, this the shit right here that's gon' help you get it. So is you still down?" Slick asked as he pulled the drugs out the bag.

"No question."

"Aight then, sit back and pay attention as I run this shit down to you one last time. This right here is crack." Slick said, as he held up an ounce of crack cocaine. "It's what the crack heads gon' be wanting. And this right here is dope – "

"And it's what the dope fiends gon' be need'n" Lil J said, finishing off Slicks last statement.

"Right, that shows me that you do be pay'n attention to some of the shit I be tell'n you."

"I pay attention to everything you tell me. I just be slipping' sometime."

"Yeah, well it might have something to do wit' that weed you be smokin'!" Slick said as he dipped back in the room to grab his utensil's. "Aight come in the kitchen so I can show you how to hook this shit up. We gon' start off wit' the crack first."

After about an hour and a half of schooling Lil J, Slick managed to show him how to breakdown, mix, and bag up an ounce of crack and 5 grams of dope.

"Don't fa'get these dimes, so don't let nobody trick you, and don't serve nobody that you ain't never seen before. This gon' be the first and last time I put you on like this, so if you fall off, that's on you. And the apartment complex that you stay in is a gold mine, so that's where you should try to move yo shit at. And don't let this little money you about to start getting stop you from go'n to school, because if you do, then I'ma have to come take it away from you – aight?" Slick asked as he paused to make sure that Lil J understood him.

"Aight."

"One more thing, I know a few smokers that live in yo building, so if you want a spot where you can chill, and get money at the same time, let me know; but for now, go out there and get a feel of the streets."

After Slick put Lil J on, he sat back in the cut and watched him hug the block and never looked back. Lil J had started seeing more money than he had ever saw in his life, and every time he sold out, he would go to Slick to re-up. Slick used to have to call one of his connects all the way out west to cop, because the niggas in Harvey was scared to sell him weight, because he had tainted his name by robbing niggas. But after he had his connect make a few phone calls to put in a good word for him, he managed to get hooked-up with a Mexican connect on the Dark Side in Harvey.

A few years later, Lil J was still doing his thang; he put his guys down on his team, and they was all getting money.

Slick was still on the run, so he was lay'n low as usual. He had fell back a little bit on robbing niggas every since he put Lil J on; and even though he had bought Lil J a .38 to protect his self if something was to ever jump off, he still found his self posted up in the cut, watching over him because he knew just how snaked-out the other niggas on the block was.

When the summer of '98 came, everything seemed to be going good. Lil J and his guys had bought cars, and was living like neighborhood supa' stars.

Slick was still doing him, and the niggas on the block was still hating, and showing envy; but they knew better than to pull something, because Slick had let it be known that he was gone go all out if something was to happen to Lil J. But all of that changed when the U.S. Marshalls came and popped Slick.

It was the middle of September, and Slick was at his girl Boo Boo's apartment, fucking and getting high all night. When he fell asleep at three in the morning, he wasn't out for no more than 30 minutes before he was awoken by the sound of the front door being kicked in. He reached under his pillow for his bull dog, and panicked when he didn't feel it, until he remembered that he left it on the dresser where he was getting high at. By the time he got to the dresser where his gun was at, the U.S. Marshall's was already bursting through the door with their guns drawn, telling him to put his hands up, and to get on the floor. Slick knew that he was a dead man no matter what he did, so he took his chances and went for his gun. But before he was able to turn around, he was knocked to the floor from the impact of the .45 that one of the Marshalls was shooting.

Boo Boo started screaming out of control when she saw Slick hit the floor, and was about to rush to his aid, but thought better of it once she saw that one of the Marshalls had his gun trained on her.

The next morning when word got back to Lil J about what happened, he immediately rushed to the police station, and was told that Slick was at the hospital. When he got to the hospital he was informed that Slick had just come out of surgery, and was in the ICU and was not allowed to see any visitors; so he left the hospital bemused in a ball of rage. When he got back to the hood, he couldn't think straight, so he fell back.

After a few days of trying to get his mind right, Lil J went to see Boo Boo to try to figure out what the hell was going on. He never knew that Slick was on the run, so when Boo Boo told him, he was surprised. He was a little upset that Slick had kept him in the dark to what was going on, but he felt better, and his head was a little clearer now that he knew what was up.

There was a rumor floating around the hood that Skip, one of the haters on the block, had called in and tipped the authorities to Slick's where abouts. Boo Boo had heard the rumor, but didn't know how true it was, so she really didn't want to tell Lil J because she didn't want him to go out and do something crazy, knowing that it was a possibility that the rumor wasn't true. So when she told him, she made him promise her that he would hold-off on going to confront Skip until she got the rumor confirmed by Slick.

Lil J made the promise and left Boo Boo's apartment knowing that he was gone break it if she didn't get in touch with Slick soon.

When he got back to the block, he saw that some of his guys was posted up doing them. Zep and Mikey was standing under the stairs in the cut smoking a blunt, and Reggie and X was on the sidewalk pitching quarters for dollars, and Black and Zed wasn't nowhere in sight.

"Ay where Black and Zed at?" Lil J asked as he approached Zep and Mikey.

"They walked up to the corner store to get somethin' to munch on." Mikey said as he grabbed the blunt from Zep.

"Who got the eight?"

"Black still got it."

Lil J shook his head. "I thought I told ya'll to leave the banger on the block wit' somebody when ya'll leave."

"That be that nigga Black; he be hold'n on to it like it's his, and don't be want'n to give it to nobody.

"I'ma have to holla at him about this shit before it become a problem. But anyway, I just heard some bullshit that we need to holla about."

"Some bull shit about what?" Zep inquired.

"About some foul shit that snake ass nigga Skip did. I just got word that he ratted out my man Slick to them people."

"Ratted him out – about what?" Mikey asked with an addled look on his face.

"He ratted him out about some bodies that –"

"Here come his bitch ass right now." Zep said cutting Lil J off.

When Lil J turned around, he saw that Skip was coming towards him with three of his guys.

"Ay Shorty, check this out, yo time on this block has expired." Skip said as he approached Lil J. "But since I been see'n you and yo guys out here grinding hard, I gotta proposition for you."

Lil J cursed his self for not having his banger on him because he had a feeling that Skip was gonna pull some bullshit now that Slick was gone but he just didn't expect him to pull it this soon. He thought about what Slick said about always expecting the unexpected, and didn't want to show any signs of weakness. So as Skip was still running off at the mouth about his proposition, he stood firm.

"Ay man hol' up." Lil J said cutting Skip off. "Who the fuck is you to be tell'n me about my time expiring on this block? Nigga you don't run shit over here."

"Shorty you need to slow down before you get what you ain't look'n for. I was try'na give you a play so that ya'll could still get money over here since – "

"What the fuck you mean you was try'na give him a play so that we could still get money over here?" X said cutting Skip off as him and Reggie walked-up and caught the ass end of the conversation. "Yo' Lil J, what this nigga talking about?"

"I don't know, but he com'n over here try'na lay his lick down like we gon' tuck our tails, and run like some bitches since Slick gone."

"Dude, Slick wasn't no fucking body; and y'all a still be getting' put off the block even if he wasn't gone."

Lil J caught the getting put off the block jab and let it go over his head. "Slick had to be somebody the way you ran yo scary ass to them people and ratted him out."

"Shorty, you don't know what you talk'n about. So I advise you to watch yo fuck'n mouth." Skip said as he began to fill with rage. Hearing Lil J put him out there made him feel more of a rat than he felt when he called in and ratted Slick out.

He was cool with Slick at first, but he had stopped liking him ever since Lil J jumped down on the scene and started taking money out of his pockets. He wanted to get down on Lil J and take his shit, but Slick let it be known that it wasn't happening, so he beared with it because he knew that Slick was crazy, and even worse when off the D.

But ever since he got word from his cousin out west that Slick was on the run, and called in to them people to get him off the streets and out of his way, he felt like he couldn't be stopped now, and was ready to get the block back in order; but Lil J was try'na taint his name and stop his show.

"Man – fuck you" Lil J started, but was cut-off as Skip delivered a right hook that caught him in the mouth and made him stumble.

When Skip tried to advance, Mikey stopped him with a left right that landed him on his ass. Tim, J.D., and Von tried to rush to his aid when they saw him hit the ground, but got tied-up as X, Reggie, and Zep squared up with them, and got it cracking.

While Skip was on the ground getting stomped out by Lil J and Mikey, he managed to pull-out his .357 and fired three shots. The first shot caught Lil J in the stomach and knocked him off his feet. The second went flying wild, and as Mikey was trying to get out the line of fire, he caught the third slug to the side of his leg and fell to the ground.

Skip got up furious, and just as he was about to train his gun on Lil J and end his career, killa Black came around the corner with Zed and started firing wild shots.

Skip, being caught off guard by the shots, immediately fled the scene after dumping his last three shells at Black.

"Ay Mikey, what the fuck happened?" Zed asked.

"Fuck what happened, go get the car. We gotta get Lil J to the hospital."

When Lil J and Mikey got to the hospital, the nurses immediately rushed Lil J into the operating room and began to perform surgery on him. After cutting him open and finding out that none of his main organs was hit, and that there was no internal bleeding, they zipped him back up, and kept him for a few days. Mikey ended up only having a flesh wound, so the doctors patched him up and released him after he fed the police a bullshit story about what happened.

On the first night in the hospital, Lil J was sitting back in pain mad as hell at hisself for almost letting a square ass nigga like Skip take him out. Boo Boo had came to see him as soon as he came out of surgery, and when she saw that he was "ok", she snapped on him for letting his self get shot. She had taking a liking to him, the same way that Slick had, and when she heard that he got shot, she was scared out of her mind.

When she got done snapping on him, she let him know that Slick was transferred to the county jail, and was in the Division 8 Medical Unit.

Before she left, she told him that she was going to see Slick the next day, and would be back to see him the following day after.

His guys came to see him on his second day in the hospital, and told him that Skip's guys was still in the hood, but Skip wasn't nowhere to be found. He told them that he wanted them to fall back, and let them know that Skip was probably somewhere lay'n low thinking that they was gonna snitch on him.

When the third day came, and he was waiting on the nurses to finish-up with his paperwork so that he could leave, he couldn't help but think about what Slick was gonna say about him letting Skip's scary ass get down on him. He just knew that he was gone be in for another one of Slick's mentor to protégé speeches, and smiled to hisself when he thought about the last one that him and Slick had. It was about a week before Slick got popped, and they was watching the Denver Broncos play the St. Louis Rams.

Slick wasn't really feeling the game anymore because he was riding with the Rams, and they were getting blown out, so he sparked up a conversation with Lil J about some shit that he wasn't feeling.

"Lil J, why is it that every time you leave the block you don't never have yo burner wit' you?"

"Because I don't be need'n it."

"What make you think you don't be need'n it?"

"Shit, I ain't got no beef wit' nobody, and you gave it to me to protect myself when I'm on the block anyway – right?"

"Hell nah, I gave it to you to protect yourself no matter where you at. And don't let me hear you say you don't need it again, because you should rather have it, and not need it, than need it, and not have it. But do you, and when you find yoself in a fucked-up situation, you gon' remember what I said."

"Boy is you ready to go, or do you wanna stay here another night?" BooBoo asked as she walked into the room and brought Lil J back from his thoughts.

"Hell nah I don't wanna stay in here, but I gotta wait for the nurse to finish wit my paperwork before I leave." Lil J said with a big cool aid smile on his face, that let BooBoo know that he was happy to see her.

"Anyway, what Slick was talk'n about yesterday when you went to see him?"

"You and that hole that you let dude put in ya ass." Boo Boo said as she grabbed the wheel chair that was by the door, and pushed it over to the bed where Lil J was lay'n.

"I got hit in the – aarrgh – stomach, not the ass." Lil J said as he winced in pain as he raised-up.

"Boy, you gotta be careful." Boo Boo said as she rushed to his aid.

"This shit hurt like a mutha-fucka."

"I bet it do, but anyway, I'm goin' to see Slick again next week, and – "

"Good, because I'm goin' wit you. I need to – "

"No you not!"

"Why?" What you don't want me ridin' wit you or something?"

"Nah, it ain't that, its just that Slick told me to take you home, and keep you on bed rest for two weeks then – "

"Two weeks? What the hell." Aw I see; yall play'n mama and daddy now huh?"

"Nah, but we can if you want us too." Boo Boo said as she gave him her best schoolgirl smile. "Anyway, Slick said to keep you in the house for two weeks, or at least until you heal-up. He also told me to let you know to be expecting some visitors."

"Some visitors – from where?"

"I don't know, but he said where they from ain't important."

☙

Out on the west side of Chicago, in Douglas Park, Slim, a light skinned, 6' 3" killa, was laid back smoking on a blunt, while a brown skinned cutie was on her knees knocking him down.

Slim was laid back at first waiting on one of his lil guys from the village to come through and scoop him up, so that they could slide out to the burbs to handle some business for one of they guys that was locked-up. But Shorty was taking too long, and Slim was getting impatient, so he occupied his self with DeDe, the brown skinned cutie, and a swisher.

DeDe was taking care of good business with the head game, and Slim was loving every minute of it, but just as he was feeling hisself about to explode all inside of her mouth, he heard a knock at the door that fucked up the whole mood. "Fuck". He mumbled to hisself as he tightened his grip around the 9mm in his right hand, and dropped the blunt in the ashtray with his left, before he pushed DeDe up off him and fixed his pants. "Go to the window and see who that is." Slim said as he grabbed the blunt out the ashtray and hit it a few times before he dipped to the back.

When DeDe got to the window and saw who it was, she screwed-up her face in disgust. "It's that little ignorant mutha-fucka that I don't like."

"Who?" Slim asked as he was coming from the back.

"That little bad mutha-fucka yall call Ed."

"Aw dats who I'm wait'n on, let him in."

DeDe walked over to the door and did as she was told, and when Lil Ed walked through the door, she sucked her teeth and walked off.

"Why you always on bullshit when I come over here?" Lil Ed asked after he closed the door and locked it.

Lil Ed was young, wild, ruthless, and really didn't care about shit. Standing 6' 1", with a smooth face, and 360s in his head, he was known in the hood as the Baby Face Gangsta.

"Because you ignorant as hell, and I don't like you." DeDe replied.

"Damn – that's how you feel?"

"Fuck dat shit G-ball, what took you so long to get over here? I told you that I wanted to get out there before it got dark so I can get familiar wit' the area." Slim said as he put the 9mm in his back pocket.

"My fault pride, but I had to smack one of my bitches up for act'n crazy, you hear me?"

"Yeah, I hear you, but I told you about beat'n-up on nem' broads. You gon' fuck around and find yo'self some where you don't wanna be."

"G, if one of my hoes ever call the police on me, I'ma kill that – "

G-ball watch yo mouth. What I tell you about talking so much? You don't know who listen'n."

Slim was starting to have second thoughts about going out to the burbs with Lil Ed, because he knew just how careless Shorty could get at times. He had already let Slick know that he really didn't want to handle no business with him because Shorty was a loose cannon; but Slick told him that Shorty was the only person other than him that he really trusted in the hood. So here Slim was, about to go out to the burbs with the Baby Face Gangsta.

"Man G, I be – "

"Fuck that shit, just remember when we get out here, I don't want you do'n no careless shit.

☙

Back at Boo Boo's apartment, Lil J was in the living room laid back on a futon watching The King of New York. He had just got off the phone with Slick, and was waiting on his so called visitors to show-up.

Slick really didn't want to talk over the phone, so Lil J didn't know what to expect of his visitors. His guys came through and dropped his .38 off, and kicked it with him for a few hours until Boo Boo told them that they had to ride.

At around eight thirty, Lil J was brought out of his doze by the phone ringing. He let it ring knowing that Boo Boo would get it sooner or later. After about four rings, Boo Boo answered it and talked for about ten seconds before she hung-up and went to the door.

Lil J gave her a dubious look, and grabbed his .38, but relaxed a little when she shook her head to let him know that everything was cool.

When Boo Boo opened the door, Slim and Lil Ed walked through it.

"What's up Boo Boo, what's go'n on wit you?" Lil Ed asked as he embraced her.

"Nuttin' I'm cool. What's up wit yo bad ass?"

"I'm good, just a lil salty about what happened to my man Slick."

"Yeah, I'm still fucked-up about it too, but he told me not to worry." Boo Boo said as she broke the embrace and turned to Slim. "You Slim – right?"

"Yeah – how you do'n?"

"I'm o'kay, what about you?"

"I'm good." Slim said before he turned his attention towards Lil J. "You Lil J?"

"Yeah, what's up?"

"Shit, you tell me, you the one wit the holes in yo ass." Slim said with a slight chuckle. "My man Slick told me that you got some problems out here."

Lil J didn't like the little comment about getting shot in the ass, but he let it go. "Something like that."

"What happened?" Lil Ed inquired.

"This coward ass nigga came on the block the other day wit his guys and tried to tell me and my guys that we had to ride. Then one thing led to another."

"Ya'll ain't have no heat out there?"

"Nah, my man was at the store wit it."

"That's crazy."

"What they call the dude that shot you?" Slim asked.

"Skip."

"Is he still in the hood?"

"Nah, my guys told me that they ain't seen him, but they say his guys still around!"

"That's good enough, but look, Slick told me that you got some loyal nigga that you can trust. One name Zed, and the other name Zep or some shit – right?"

"Yeah, but I can trust all my niggas, they all loyal."

"That might be true, but the only ones I wanna fuck wit is the ones that Slick told me about; and that's Zed and Zep. So call'em up, and have'em here in about an hour. Me and my man about to hit the streets and get familiar wit the area. When we get back, we gon' be ready to take care of business, so have yo guys ready."

୯୬

"What's up Boo Boo, how you do'n?" Zed asked as him and Zep walked through the door after Boo Boo opened it to let them in.

"I'm okay Zed, but I could be better." she replied.

Lil J looked at Zed and Zep and smiled to hisself. He had called them, and let them know he needed them within an hour, and here they were ten minutes later.

"What's up J, what the business is?" Zed asked as he walked over and greeted Lil J.

"Shit really, but a couple of goons just showed-up and they need ya'll assistance wit that lame Skip."

"Our assistance? Who deese goons suppose to be?" Zed asked.

"They some niggas that my man Slick sent through, so they good. But I need ya'll to roll wit 'em and show 'em how Skip and his people look aight?"

"Yeah, we got you, but I told you we ain't been seen dude in the hood; as a matter-of-fact we ain't seen him in the hood since the day he got down on you and Mikey." Zed said.

"Aight I understand that, but you did say you still be see'n his guys right?"

"Yeah, them clowns still be on the black."

"That's good because them niggas gotta get it too; and the way they chill'n on the block like everything good ain't gon' do nutt'n but make them niggas easier to get."

"So what these so called goons got planned for Skip and his guys?"

"I don't know, but ya'll gon' soon find out. But like I said before, these Slick guys. I don't know'em from a can of paint, so I want ya'll to be carefull out there wit'em. Lil J said as he pulled the .38 out of his front pocket and handed it to Zed.

"Here, take the eight, just bring it back to me later."

Lil J spent a hour and twenty minutes hollering at Zed and Zep before Boo Boo was opening the front door to let Slim and Lil Ed back in.

Slim and Lil Ed had rode around for a hour and a half getting familiar with the streets and was now ready to take care of business, so they could head back out west.

"Which one of ya'll is Zed?" Slim asked as he looked from Zed who had long braids hanging down his back, to Zep who had deep ocean waves that were so thick, they made Lil Ed's waves look like ripples.

"I am, what's happen'n?" Zed asked as he sized Slim and Lil Ed up.

"Did ya man let ya'll know what the business was?"

"Yeah, he put us up on game, and let us know that ya'll need our assistance."

"Nah see that's where he wrong at, we don't need shit, because we ain't the ones wit the problems. Ya'll need our assistance." Lil Ed said as he walked over to the futon, and took a seat next to Lil J, who was now sitting upright.

"You done Pride?" Slim asked.

Lil Ed didn't respond, he just looked at Slim with a smirk on his face that some considered to be his trademark smile.

"Anyway, from my understanding, ya'll say that ya'll ain't been see'n dude who shot ya man right?"

"Nah, we ain't been see'n that nigga." Said Zed. "But his guys still be in the hood."

"How many of 'em is it?"

"Three."

"You think they out there right now?"

"Shit, two of 'em was out there before we came over here, but that was almost two hours ago."

"Aight look, let me run something down to ya'll real quick before we hit the streets." Slim said as he began to put Zed and Zep up on game.

Thirty minutes later, Slim, Lil Ed, Zed, and Zep were parked in a cut watching Von and J.D., who was posted on the block like they were holding the fort down. Tim wasn't anywhere in sight, so they suspected that he was probably in one of the apartments with a broad, or maybe chilling with Skip who was hiding out.

"What up wit these two lames? What they be on?" Lil Ed asked referring to Von and J.D.

"They really don't be on shit," said Zep. "I mean look at 'em. These clowns been out here for more than ten years and ain't on shit. Mu' fucka's still nickel and dimin'; and to make it so bad, this block was dead before we started gett'n money over here. This bitch wasn't even do'n three hundred a night. Now we got it do'n more than three stacks a night."

While Lil Ed and Zep were conversing, Slim was laid back deep in his thoughts while simultaneously watching the block. He liked and respected the way Lil J and his guys were trying to come up, but what he detested was how these over grown ass niggas were trying to stop them from shining. He guessed that somebody forgot to tell Skip that if he didn't get what he had been trying to get by now, he wasn't going to get it.

Slim had seen a lot of niggas lose their life to up and coming shorties in the hood. Shorties that were hungry and determined to get it without letting nothing or no one stand in their way. He also saw some of those same shorties fall victim to the streets because someone forgot to forewarn them about the dangers in which the streets held.

"Ay Zed, my man Slick told me that you and you lil' brother the realest niggas outta ya'll circle next to Lil J." Slim said while still observing the block. "I'ma put ya'll up on a lil game that's gon' make ya'll some serious hitters if ya'll choose to listen. Now I think ya'll know that this a dangerous game that ya'll play'n, and only the strong and smart survive. And always remember that this just a game so never let ya'll feelings get involved."

Slim and Lil Ed spent the next few days showing Zed and Zep how to professionally watch Von and J.D., while dropping game on them at the same time. They were hoping that Skip would show-up or that one of his guys would lead them to him, but unfortunately that didn't happen, and Slim was getting impatient, so he decided to go with plan "B".

"Ay G-ball, make sho' you be on bidness because I ain't try'na be play'n wit' these niggas." Slim said as he checked his gun to make sure that it was cocked. Him and Lil Ed were in the alley on the side of the apartment buildings getting ready to make their move.

☙

Von and J.D. were sitting on the stairs smoking a blunt with Tasha, a bus'd chick that they were trying to run through before the night ended. They had already smoked three blunts with her, and were ready to get their fuck on, but Tasha wasn't ready yet. She knew that they had some more weed, and wanted to smoke as much as she could before she laid-up with them.

"Tasha baby what's up? is you ready to show me and my man what that thang do or what?" Von asked after he passed the blunt to J.D.

"Nigga I keep tell'n you that this thang might be too much for you and ya man to handle." Tasha stated.

"Shit, the way you stall'n make me think that it might be the other way around." J.D. said after he exhaled the smoke out of his mouth.

"Boy pleze, I – "

Was as far as Tasha got before Slim and Lil Ed came from behind the stairs with their guns drawn.

"Bitch, if you scream it's gon, be the last thing you do." Said Slim.

"Ay man, what ya'll on?" Von said trying not to show that he was terrified.

"Shut the fuck up and put ya hands on yo head and come off the stairs."

As the three of them put their hands on their heads and were coming down the stairs like they were told, J.D. thought about going for his gun, but thought better of it when he saw the murder in Slim's eyes.

"Face the fucking wall!" Slim ordered.

"Man if it's – "

Crack!

"Shut the fuck up!" Lil Ed snapped, after he smacked J.D. across his shit with a .40 and knocked him to the ground.

"Now get yo punk ass back up before I put some holes in yo ass."

"G-ball, hurry up and search these mu'fucka's so we can bounce." Slim said as he gave Zed and Zep the signal letting them know to bring the Chevy around.

"Whoa G, this nigga was hold'n. Check this out." Lil Ed said referring to the .38 snubnose that he pulled off of J.D.

Zed pulled up in the alley just in time to see Slim stuffing the .38 into his pocket.

"Ay one of ya'll come help my man check these mu' fucka's." Slim said without taking his eyes off the trios.

"I already searched dude, just come check this bitch real quick." Lil Ed said to Zed who was walking up.

While Zed was searching Tasha, J.D. looked out the corner of his eye, and damn near shit himself when he saw who the third person was. The reality of the situation hit him in the face like a sledge hammer. "Fuck." He said to hisself wishing that he would have tried his luck when he thought about going for his gun.

"Ay shorty, grab that bitch and put her in the backseat while we put these niggas in the trunk." Said Slim.

"We really don't need this bitch do we?" Zed asked but regretted it as soon as the words left his mouth.

Slim didn't even respond. He just shot Zed a look that let him know that right now wasn't the time for twenty one questions.

"We ain't even – "

Crack!

Von started but was cut-off from a blow to the back of the head that sent him to his knees.

"Shut the fuck up, this ain't the time for that shit!" Lil Ed snapped as he grabbed Von by his hoodie and pulled him back to his feet. "Now get yo dumb ass in that trunk before I shoot yo stupid ass."

Fifteen minutes after Von, J.D., and Tasha were kidnapped, they found themselves tied-up inside the basement of an abandoned house with Slim, Lil Ed, Zed, and Zep standing over them with flashlights.

Tasha didn't know what was going on and hoped like hell that this was just a bad dream.

Von and J.D. knew what was up and prayed that they would be able to talk their way out of it if they were ever given the chance.

"You niggas already know what's up, so we aint' got time for ya'll to be play'n stupid." Slim said as he bent down in between Von and J.D.

Tasha started shaking her head and trying to talk, but everything she said came out muffled. Slim thought about taking the duct tape off her mouth so that he would be able to understand what she was trying to say, but disregarded it.

"Baby girl I know you don't know what's go'n on, but unfortunately you was in the wrong place at the wrong time." Slim said before turning his attention back to Von and J.D. "Anyway, I need one of you niggas to tell me where I can find Skip." They both shook their heads.

"I just told ya'll that we ain't got time for ya'll to be play'n stupid. Now I'ma ask ya'll again…do ya'll know where I can find Skip?" This time only J.D. shook his head.

"Okay, have it ya'll way. Grab this mu'fucka right here and duct tape his ass to that pole over there. And make sho'ya'll take his shoes off first. I'ma 'bout to make this bitch wish he was never born." Slim said as he walked over and grabbed a ball ping hammer from Zep who was holding the bag of supplies.

While Zed and Lil Ed were duct taping J.D. to the pole, he was still fuming with himself for getting caught slipping. He knew that whatever they were about to do to him was going to be painful, but he planned on taking it like a soldier.

Von on the other hand, was praying and hoping that J.D. would fold so he wouldn't have to. He just couldn't bear the thought of being tortured, but little did he know, his time would soon come.

"I'ma give yo punk ass one more chance to tell me where dis nigga at." Slim said as he snatched the duct tape off of J.D.'s mouth.

"How the fuck I'm 'pose to tell you something that I don't know?"

"I don't know, but we about to find out. Here G-ball, show these lil niggas how to make a mu' fucka spill his guts."

"Aight G, hold this light." Lil Ed said as he grabbed the hammer and went to work.

"Aaaaagggghhhh!" J.D hollered as one of this toes was crushed.

"Aaaaagggghhhh!"

"Hold up G-ball, see if that nigga ready to talk." Slim said as he pointed the flash light into J.D.'s face.

Lil Ed raised up and looked J.D. in his eyes expecting to see fear, but he didn't. What he saw was a man that was trying to protect his image by standing firm and not folding on his man; and he knew that it was going to take more than smashing a few toes to get him to talk.

God damn this shit hurt, but I ain't about to fold because these bitches gon' kill me anyway, and I'll be damned if I go out like a bitch, J.D. thought to himself.

"Ay man, you might as well tell us where this nigga at so we can gone and get this shit over with." said Lil Ed.

Haktwoo "Nigga fuck you!" J.D. said as he spit in Lil Ed's face.

Lil Ed instantly became enraged and started swinging the hammer wildly at J.D.

Crack. Crack. Crack. Crack.

Stop G, hold on!" Slim hollered.

Crack. Crack.

"G, hold the fuck up!" Slim said as he grabbed the bloody hammer from Lil Ed.

Lil Ed had blood all over him and was breathing hard trying to catch his breath.

"Fuck this nigga G. He spit in my face." Lil Ed said still fuming.

"G, you got blood all over you. That's evidence. And look what you did to this nigga. How the fuck we suppose to get him to talk now?"

Lil Ed looked over to J.D. and saw that he was unconscious, and then looked over to Von.

"G, fuck dude, he wasn't gon' talk anyway, so I did us a favor by gett'n him out of the way."

This one stupid mu'fucka man. I knew I shouldn't have brought his crazy ass out here with me. He be doing too much. Now if we get pulled over or anything, this mu'fucker gonna have blood all over him and get us popped. Fuck this shit, that nigga got one more time to do something stupid and I'ma change his ass. I ain't about to lose my freedom because of him.

"G, untie this nigga and drag him back over there by that bitch. Shorty, you and ya man grab that other nigga and tie him up to this pole." Slim said to Zed.

"You want his shoes off?" Zed asked.

"Yeah, and bring me them tooth picks out of that bag too." Slim said as he walked over to J.D. and wiped the hammer off on his shirt.

Slim didn't like the way that Lil Ed handled the situation with J.D. because it allowed him to get off easy, so he planned on taking care of Von hisself so that they could get the information that they needed before getting rid of him.

After Zed and Zep finished duct taping Von to the pole, Slim walked up and shined the light in his face, blinding him.

"By the time I get done with yo ass you gon' be begging me to let you spill yo guts." Slim said before he passed his flash light to Lil Ed and grabbed the tooth picks from Zep.

Twenty minutes later Von was feeling worse than he looked. Slim had hammered toothpicks underneath all ten of his toe nails, and cut both sides of his face with a box cutter before pouring salt in his wounds.

The torturing that Slim did to Von was unnecessary because he was ready to spill his guts after he saw Lil Ed beat J.D. unconscious with the hammer.

"I'ma 'bout to take this tape off yo mouth so you can tell me what the fuck I wanna know. But if you spit on me, I'm not gon' kill you or beat you unconscious, I'm just gon' put the tape back on yo mouth, and start the torturing over. Now you don't want that do you?"

Von shook his head vigorously.

"Aight then, make me a believer." Slim said as he snatched the tape off Von's mouth and listened as the tortured man started telling him everything that he wanted to hear and more. When Von was finished, Slim knew everything. Where Skip was hiding out at, how many niggas was with him, how many bitches, how many guns, drugs, and money. The only thing that he didn't know was how many dishes were in the sink.

"G, I'ma 'bout to fuck this bitch before we ride." Lil Ed said as he flashed the light on Tasha.

"Hell nah G, you know I ain't with that goofy ass shit."

"G-ball, I ain't – "

"G, this shit ain't open for discussion, so pack that shit up and lets ride. Shorty, I want ya'll to cut they throats and hit 'em in the head before we ride."

"What about her?" Zep asked as he pointed to Tasha.

"Shorty I told you that this a dangerous game, and if you planning on surviving, then you gon' have to man up. We don't leave no witnesses." Slim said as he pulled the .38 out of his pocket and handed it to him. "Now take care of yo business."

"Come on man I swear I won't say – " was as far as Von got before Zed put a hole in his head.

After Zep saw his brother take care of Von, he went and took care of Tasha and J.D.

☙

Out in Dolton, Skip and Tim were chilling, getting fucked-up over a broad named Tia's house. Tia was best friends with Sabrina who was there to keep Tim company, so that her and Skip could do whatever they chose to do without being bothered. Skip could have easily kicked Tim out, but he liked keeping him around, sort of like a bodyguard.

At the moment they were all in the kitchen playing dirty hearts for apple vodka and were smoking on an ounce of some garbage ass weed. They were so messed-up and into their card game that they never heard the four killers that were in the living room, until it was too late.

Slim was the first one to enter the kitchen and he came in blasting followed by Lil Ed. Zed and Zep were checking the other rooms, but by the time they made it to the kitchen, it was a blood bath. Four bodies were laid-out, and all of them were lifeless save for Skip who was barely breathing.

"Shorty man....what the fuck?" Skip asked.

"You know what's up nigga." Zed said before he walked up and put a bullet in Skip's head.

Early the next morning, Lil J was awakened out of his sleep by Boo Boo who was watching the seven o'clock news. She was just about to leave the house on her way to work when the top story caught her attention. It was a quadruple murder that happened two suburbs away from Harvey. At first she thought it was probably an act of random violence until she saw the pictures of the four victims.

"John... John look. Ain't that the boy that shot you?" Boo Boo asked, pointing to the T.V.

Lil J looked at the T.V. and blinked his eyes a few times trying to make sure that he was seeing correctly before the pictures disappeared. He became excited from what he had just seen, and wanted to jump up out of the bed and celebrate, but he refrained because he didn't want to get Boo Boo all worked-up. He couldn't believe it, he had just seen Skip, Tim, and two females on the news in a quadruple homicide. He didn't know who the females were, but he was a hundred and ten percent sure that the two guys were Skip and Tim.

"John, was that him?" Boo Boo asked again, catching Lil J off guard.

"Huh?"

"Was that the boy that shot you?"

"Aw nah." Lil J responded before he laid back down. He was trying to holdback the excitement that was building inside of him.

Boo Boo looked at him like he was crazy because she knew that he was lying. She wanted to press the issue, but was already late for work; so she just made a mental note to grill him later about it before she got up and left.

Lil J waited until he heard the door slam and the locks click before he got up and called Zed. He not only wanted to get the four one on what happened, he wanted to let Zed and the rest of his guys know that it was time to make a point; and that point was that Lil J and his crew weren't to be fucked with under no circumstances. But little did he know, the point was already made because the news about what happened to Skip was already spreading through the hood.

CHAPTER 5

    Down on the other end of the projects, Mack and Rob were sitting back in the cut blowing on some kush with Lil Bill, Murda, B.C., Red and Gary; five of their wildest young soldiers. They had just come back from Harvey thirty minutes ago. They were out there riding through Lil J's block waiting for him to show up, until they got a call from Tone letting them know that Tank was calling a meeting back in the projects. So now they were back in the hood waiting on Tank and Tone to show up.

    "I wonder what's taking Tank and them so long?" Murda asked after he finished rolling up another blunt.

    "Be easy lil bruh, you know Tank ain't to be rushed." Mack said before he grabbed the blunt from Rob, that was already burning.

    "I know, but I just can't believe that this nigga Lil J still breathing after the way he got down on our guys."

    "It ain't like a mu'fucka ain't been tryna get at him." Mack said after he inhaled the weed smoke out of his mouth.

    "I mean, Lil Bill brother poked his ass up at court back in '06, but the bitch ass nigga just didn't die."

    "So what time you think we gone make it back out to Harvey?"

    "I don't know, but if this meeting don't last long we should be back out there in no time." Mack said before he hit the blunt a few more times and passed it to B.C. After he inhaled the smoke, he looked around at the five young soldiers. He knew that they were the hardest and realest soldiers they had; and that was the reason he begirded himself with them.

    They were going to ride or die to the end. And if something was ever to happen to him, Tank, Tone, or Rob, he knew that they had the brains and the heart to step up and hold the projects down without letting it crumble.

"Ay, here come them niggas now." Red said, bringing Mack back from this thoughts.

When Mack turned around he saw Tank and Tone walking up. "What up Tank? What's happening?"

"What's happening, - nigga I tell ya'll to grab a few of the troops and go out to Harvey, and ya'll take all of the main hitters. What's up with that?" Tank asked as he walked up and grabbed the blunt out of B.C.'s hand.

"What, you wanted us to take some of them other half way ass gangsta's out there with us?

"Nah I ain't saying that, but if ya'll got all the main hitters out there with ya'll, then who the hell gon' be here to guide these clowns, if and when them niggas from the new projects come through?"

"Shit, we left Steve and A.P. out here."

Tank laughed as he exhaled the smoke out of his mouth.

"What, you try'n to be funny nigga? You know them niggas ain't good for shit but getting money, so stop playing. The next time ya'll go out to Harvey, leave B.C and Gary here and take some of them other niggas with ya'll.

"Aight, we got you, don't trip."

"What was going on when ya'll was out there anyway? Did that nigga show up?"

"Nah, but – "

Boom!Boom!Boom! Boom! was the sound that cut Mack off.

"Damn, I bet that's them niggas from the new." Tank said as he pulled out his 44. Automatic. "Mack, you and Rob take Murda, Bill, and B.C and go to the other end of the projects. Red and Gary, ya'll come with me. Let's ride Tone.

☙

When X pulled up to the Vail Apartments, Reggie and three of the workers stepped out of the cut and approached the truck.

"What's up jo?" What's happening?" Reggie asked as he watched Lil J climb out of the truck clutching a fifth of Rosé in his left hand, and a .45 in his right.

"I'm whats happening nigga. I'm back!" Lil J said as him and Reggie embraced.

"Yeah, I see you done got a lil bigger up in there."

"That come from eating good." Lil J said as he patted his stomach.

"You better been eating good up in there with all of that money we was sending yo ass."

"Yeah, you niggas did make sho' I was good, even tho' I was good already."

"Ay let's go up to the spot before them people pull up and pop us out here with these thangs." said Zed.

"Mikey, grab my other banger and the rest of that liquor out the truck for me." Lil J said as him and his guys made their way up to the spot.

The "spot" was a three bedroom apartment inside of the complex building that Lil J and his guys were holding down. It was used for chilling, getting fucked-up, and counting money. They also had a few other spots where they chopped-up drugs and kept guns.

Lil J's empire was still standing firm because he was a strong and smart leader. He organized his guys and put them in positions where he saw that they fit. He had Reggie, Mikey and X handling the money and drugs, and Zed, Zep, and K.B. handling the guns and security, while he sat back and made sure that everything was secure. Reggie was in the key position to oversee the drugs and money. He made sure that everybody got an equal chop every month after he paid the workers and put up the re-up money.

Zed was also in a key position. He oversaw the guns and security. He made sure that the guns and shooters were on location at all times. He also put extra workers down on security so that when him, Zep or K.B. wasn't there, somebody would still be there to make sure that the block was secure.

As they entered the spot, Lil J and Mikey popped the bottles.

"So what's up Lil J? We gon' call some hoe's up and do it big or what?" Reggie inquired as Mikey passed him a cup that was mixed with Remy and Rosé.

"Nah, not right now. We got business to take care of first. I know you heard about the hits that Rick got out on me."

"Yeah, I know all about that shit. But nigga you just came home. We can put some more security out there and do us tonight. Then tomorrow we can take care of business."

"That sounds like a plan Reggie." said Zed. "But the shit that's going on seriouser than you think. We got these snake ass stick-up niggas waiting to take us out, and you know them niggas from Robbins gon' be hitting the block even harder then they was before now that they know that Lil J back on the scene."

"You know what? Now that you brought that up, the workers have been telling me that some niggas been riding through here looking crazy. It might've been them niggas from Robbins. I didn't think nothing of it at first because ain't nobody been coming through the block on bullshit in awhile, but now that I think about it, it might've been them niggas."

"What – "

"When was the last time they came through? Lil J asked, cutting Zed off.

"I don't know, but the workers told me this at about three o'clock."

"Damn Zed, you starting to fall off ain't you. I mean you used to be on top of shit like this – "

"And I still am!" Zed said, cutting Lil J off. "I just got the workers reporting to Reggie or whoever on the block when I'm not around. But believe me, if some niggas been coming through here on bullshit, the workers on point and ready to do whatever. You know I'm gone make sho' that the security tight. Watch this." he said as he grabbed his phone and hollered through the chirp. "JJ, put Ant in charge and come up to the "spot".

"I'm on my way." came back through the chirp.

"J.J., Ant, you put them lil niggas on security?" Lil J inquired.

"Yeah, I had to rearrange the workers and put niggas where they belonged. I even had to get rid of some niggas."

Bam. Bam. Bam

"That should be J.J. at the door. Mikey, check and make sho' before you let him in." said Zed.

Mikey pulled out his .40 before he peeked out the window. When he opened the door, J.J. stepped in.

What the fuck, J.J. thought to hisself as he looked at the guns on the table to the .40 in Mikey's hand. He knew that he hadn't done anything wrong, so he spoke up.

"What up Zed – everything cool?"

"Yeah, everything cool, I just need you to clear something up for me. What type of heat you hold'n right now?"

"Two thirty shot .45s"

"What the – "

"Thirty shot .45s? let me see them bitches." Lil J said cutting Zed off.

J.J. reached behind his back and pulled out two all black glocks with extended clips, and handed them to Lil J.

"Damn Zed." Lil J said, admiring the guns.

"Why I ain't got none of these?"

"Nigga, it's more where them came from. But we can holler about that shit later. J.J. what the soldiers out there holding?"

"Mac' 11s, Techs, and .45s. We got a few Ks, and ARs out there too.

"Tell me what's up with this shit I'm hearing about niggas coming through the block."

"Some niggas came through here earlier about four different times in three different whips."

"Was it the same niggas every time or different mu'fuckers?"

"It was different mu'fuckers, but the same niggas."

"What the fuck you mean it was different mu'fuckers but the same niggas?" X inquired a little addled.

"I mean it was different mu'fuckers, but the same niggas. Like they was from the same hood or something because every time they came through, it was different mu'fuckers except for one nigga. If it wasn't for him I would've thought it was different niggas."

"So you saying that he came through every time?"

"Yeah, but we on them niggas tho. We just waiting on them to make one wrong move so we can chop they ass up."

"Aight look" said Zed. "I'ma come holler at you in a minute to get some more info on them niggas. But right now I need you to go out there and stand back on the security. Make sho' that ya'll don't let noboady come through here without checking them out first. I don't give a fuck who it is. If something go down make sho' you hit me on the chirp.

"Aight I got you."

"These some nice bangers lil nigga, but they ain't shit if you don't know how to use 'em." Lil J said as he wiped his finger prints off the guns and set them on the table.

J.J. picked his guns up and left without saying another word.

"I like that lil nigga, but can he be trusted?" Lil J inquired.

"Yeah he can be trusted. That's why I put him on security. Him, Ant, Mall, and B the realest workers we got, they kinda remind me of how we used to be."

"Ay I know what I wanted to ask ya'll." Lil J said changing the subject. "Whatever happened to the witnesses on my case? I thought ya'll said ya'll couldn't find them."

"Shit we couldn't." Zed said until he thought about what Lil J was really asking. "Wait; I hope you don't think we had something to do with them niggas disappearing?"

"So what you saying – ya'll didn't?"

"Hell nah we didn't. The last time we saw them niggas they was out in the old projects. At first we was keeping up with them waiting on you to give us the green light. Then all of a sudden they just disappeared."

"How long has it been since ya'll last seen them?"

"Like five months."

"I think it might be something else to that shit. Them niggas didn't just disappear for nothing, because if that was the case then them niggas wouldn't have came to court on me in the first place."

"With the way Rick sending hits, I wouldn't be surprised if it's something else to that shit either."

"I want you to check into that shit later aight?"

"I got you."

"Ay Mikey, when was the last time you went to check on my O.G.?"

"I went to see her the other day. She was having problems with her car so I took it to the shop. Everything cool with her tho', she told me to make sure that I tell you to come see her."

"Aight I'ma go see her, but what's up with my whips while you taken cars to the shop and shit?" Lil J asked referring to his cars. He had a Dodge Charger with a Hemi in it, a CTS Cadillac, and a 85 Cutlas. All of them was leathered out with 22s on them save for the Cutlass. It was leathered out sitting on 24s with T tops.

"I been taking care of yo shit man. They in the storage, but we can go get 'em in the morning."

"Nah fuck them cars, we going to the lot. I wanna grab me one of them 645 Coupes."

"Aw yeah, them bitches hot right now too."

"I know, I'ma bang that mu'fucka out, and throw some Ds on Dat Bitch!" Lil J said as they all laughed.

While they were still laughing, Reggie dipped into one of the back rooms and came back with a bag. "Here go that Evisu Fit and them Pradas you called and told me to go get the other day, and here go yo phone."

"Aight good looking bruh. but where that new PS3 at? I know ya'll got it."

"Come on man, you know damn well Mikey went and bought that shit and almost every game that come out to that mu' fucka." said X.

"Man – fuck you." Mikey said as he refilled his cup.

"I bet he put one of 'em in every spot didn't he?" Lil J asked.

"Hell yeah. That nigga crazy." said Reggie.

"Mikey hook it up and let me see what's to that live 07."

"That shit the business. But it's hard to play if you don't know what you doing. So you might have some problems."

"Aight. Ay Zed, hit Zep and K.B. up and see what's going on with them stick-up niggas."

CHAPTER 6

Out in Midlothian, Zep and K.B. were laid back in a Dodge Mini Van keeping an eye on Donta, Tray and Los. They had been watching them since six o'clock, around the time that Zed, Mikey and X went to pickup Lil J. But that was almost four hours ago, and they were getting tired of waiting on Donta and his guys to come out of a crib that they had dipped off into about two hours ago.

"These lame ass niggas need to hurry up and come up out of there. I don't know why Zed ain't just give us the ok to get rid of these mu'fuckas." K.B. fumed.

"Be easy killa. I wanna get rid of these clowns just as bad as you do. But we gotta have patience. Zed ain't give us the green light for a reason."

"So what is the use in following and watching these niggas if we ain't gon' do shit to 'em. I mean that shit don't make no sense to me."

"The shit don't make no sense to me either, but this what Zed told us to do, so this what we gon' do. If you don't like it, take that ship up with him." Zep said as his phone started vibrating. When he looked at the caller I.D. and saw Zed's number, he tried to pass the phone to K.B. "Here that nigga go right here. You wanna ask him all that shit that you was just asking me?"

"Just answer the mu' fucka and see what he want." K.B. said as he pushed the phone away.

Zep shook his head before answering the phone. "What up?"

"Ay Lil bruh, what the business is? What's up with them kids?"

"Ain't shit up with these clown ass niggas. They dipped off into some crib out here in Mid-Low, we been out here in the cut waiting on them to come out and hit the streets for like two hours."

"What up with K.B.! What he on?"

"What he on? This crazy mu'fucka bugging, that's what he on."

"Let him know I said to be easy. And tell him I got him when the time is right."

"I already told him what's up. He just on some other shit right now. But anyway what's up with Lil J?"

"He ain't really on nothing right now but chilling, drinking on some Rémy and Rosé, and playing live with Mikey."

"You put him up on what's going on in the hood.?"

"Come on now bruh, you already know that's the first thing I did."

"So what's up with him as far as that other shit?"

"You talking 'bout that soft falling back ass shit?"

"Yeah."

"Yeah, I hollered at him about it, but he say he ain't on that."

"It'll be kinda hard for him to fall back anyway with all of the shit that's going on."

"That's the same thing I was thinking, but he ain't falling back so all of that shit irrelevant."

"Aight so what's up with these niggas out here?"

"That depends on how it's looking."

"It's looking good. All we waiting on is the "ok"."

"Aight just be easy. Me and X gon' meet ya'll. –"

"Hold up!" Zep said cutting Zed off. "It look like these niggas coming out the crib right now."

"Yeah that's them." Said K.B."You should let me get out and change they ass right now.

"Hell nah be cool." Zep said to K.B before he started back talking to Zed.

"A big bruh, these niggas 'bout to hit the streets. What's up?"

"This what's up. I want ya'll to hold fast. Me and X gon' meet up with ya'll in a minute. We gon' take care of this shit together."

"Aight just hit my phone." Zep said before he ended the call.

"That nigga gave us the red light didn't he?" K.B. asked.

"Yeah, he say he gon' meet up with us so we can take care of these niggas together.

"I knew that's all he wanted was a piece of the action. That's why he stallin' us out." K.B. said as he put the van in drive.

"Look at this lame ass nigga Los. He still don't' know I be fucking his bitch." Zep said as he laid the Mossberg back on the floor.

☙

When Donta and his guys left the crib that they were chilling in out in Midlothian, they headed out to Harvey to see what was popping.

Donta and Tray were hoping to catch Lil J and his guys somewhere sweet so that they could get the shit over with and go pick-up their money. Los, on the other hand, had a bad feeling about the whole situation. He knew that if they didn't take the situation serious, it wouldn't be no picking-up money; it would be pushing up daisies. And he wasn't trying to get killed for something that he didn't have nothing to do with in the first place. So as they were headed out to Harvey, his bad feelings made him question Donta and Tray.

"Yo Donta, where we headed when we get out here?" Los inquired.

Donta lit up a blunt and hit it a few times before he responded.

"We gone slide through them niggas block to see what's popping and ride down on a few hoes to see if it's a party going on out there."

"What we gone do if we can't catch them at a party or on the block slipping?"

Donta hit the blunt a few more times before he passed it to Tray.

"Then we gone post up in the cut on they block and wait for them to show up , or catch they ass at the gas station or something."

Los took his eyes off the road to look over at Donta to see if he was serious before he snapped.

"You must be out yo mu'fuckin' mind! What you think we going to kill some kids or something?"

"Man you been acting funny lately. What the fuck wrong with you. You acting like you scared of them mu' fuckas like they some professional hitters or – "

"Nigga I ain't scared of shit. I just don't like the way ya'll sitting around talking like this shit a game, or like them niggas just gon' let us walk up and get down on them. And how them twin niggas get down, I won't be surprised if they already know that we getting paid to take out they man."

"So that's what it is. Them twin niggas got you shook the fuck up?"

"Ain't no mu' fucka got me shook." Los said as he grabbed the blunt from Tray and hit it a few times. "I don't know why we took this hit in the first place. We ain't got no problems with them niggas. And we stick-up niggas, not hit men, we just kill if the need be."

"You starting to sound like a bitch." Tray snapped. "If yo punk ass don't wanna roll with us then drop us the fuck off at the Hud. Me and Donta can jump in my whip and go take care of this shit our mu' fuckin self. All you wanna do is lay up with that bitch anyway. Nigga fuck you."

"You right, I'm just gon' drop you dumb mu' fuckas off because I ain't going out on no send off shit."

∽

Back at the spot, Lil J had stopped playing the game and hopped in the shower while Zed went out to holler at J. J. about tightening up the security on the block because him and X were about to leave, and he wanted to make sure that Lil J was well protected.

X was now playing Mikey in live while Reggie was sitting back talking on his phone.

As Lil J was coming out of the bathroom from showering and getting dressed, Zed was walking back in to let him know that he had put J. J up on what was going down.

Zed had already hollered at Lil J before he got in the shower about how they were going to handle the stick-up niggas. Lil J wanted to ride out with them, but Zed talked him into staying at the spot with Mikey and Reggie.

Lil J knew that Zed was on top of his shit, so he just fell back and let X roll out with him. He thought about going to check into a hotel, but disregarded it because he didn't want to get caught with his pants down knowing that niggas were out to get him.

"You ready?" X asked Zed as he got up and picked up his twin .40s.

"Yeah." Zed responded before he hollered through his chirp. "J.J, go get Pinkey and put her in the bubble for me."

"Aight I got you." came back through the chirp.

"Ay be careful out there, and don't foget to hit us up and let us know that ya'll good." Said Lil J.

"Aight we got you, but don't worry about us because these niggas ain't on shit." Zed said before him and X walked out the door. "So we riding out in the bubble?" X asked as him and Zed were walking down the stairs on their way to the parking lot. "Yeah, we gon' take the bubble cause Zep and K. B. already got the van."

As they approached the bubble, Zed tossed X the keys and told him to drive while he hopped in the passenger seat and looked in the back to make sure that J.J. dropped the AR-15 off like he told him to do. After he saw the AR and the two 120 round drums on the back seat, he hit Zep up to ask him his location.

"What up?" Zep asked as he picked-up on the first ring.

"Where ya'll at?" Zed asked.

"We on 147th Street. We just passed up the block."

"Damn. Which way ya'll going?"

"East towards the strip joint."

"Aight we should be beheind ya'll in like three minutes. I'ma hit you on the chirp." Zed said as he got off the phone. "X, they on 147th Street going towards the strip joint. Won't you try to catch up with them before they turn off somewhere."

"Aight." X said as he put the car in drive and pulled out of the parking lot. He took Leavitt up to 147th Street where he made a right. The speed limit was 35, but he was doing 50 until he looked up the road and saw a dark colored van that looked similar to the one that Zep and K.B. was in. "Zed, don't that look like them niggas up there?"

Zed took a second to look at the van before he spoke. "Yeah that's them." He said before hollering through his chirp. "Lil bruh, we a few cars behind ya'll."

"I already know. Ya'll in the bubble right?"

"Yeah. What type of whip them kids in?"

"They in that black boy that's a few cars in front of us. We gon' follow them and see where they going. So I want ya'll to stay back there and be cool." Zep said as they passed up the strip joint and stayed on 147th Street for a few more minutes until they saw Los put on his left turn signal.

Zep really didn't like hollering back and forth through the chirp, so he grabbed his phone and called Zed.

"What up bruh?" Zed answered on the first ring.

"It look like these niggas 'bout to go through they hood. We gon' turn off right here and come around the other way. Ya'll keep following them."

"Aight we got you." Zed said before hanging up.

As K.B and Zep turned off, X saw Los turn left at the light just as it was turning red. When he made it to the light and looked down the block, he saw that Los had stopped in the middle of the street and two people were getting out of his car.

When the light changed and X turned down the block, the car was pulling off and he noticed that the two people he saw getting out of the car were Donta and Tray. They were standing next to a parked car. Donta was standing on the passenger side while Tray was on the driver's side going through his pockets.

Zed knew that this was the perfect time to make a move, so he turned around and grabbed the AR off the back seat before hollering through his chirp. "Lil bruh, it's curtains on two ducks, but catch the last one coming yo way."

☙

When Tank, Tone, Red and Gary made it out to the parking lot, they saw that the loud booms that cut mack off weren't gun shots, they were fireworks that Tiny, Marcus, and Dolla were playing with.

Tank had a low tolerance for ignorance, and the way that Tiny, Marcus, and Dolla were playing with fireworks in the hood knowing that they were warring was definitely a sign of ignorance.

"Whoa. Whoa. Tank, what's wrong man?" Dolla asked after he turned around and saw Tank approaching them with his gun out. Tone, Red, and Gary also had their guns out too, but they were standing back posted.

"What the fuck you niggas out here playing with fireworks for knowing that it's going down?"

"Tank we ain't think – "

Crack!

"Shut the fuck up!" Tank snapped as he hit Dolla across his shit with the 44. "You niggas don't get paid to think. Ya'll get paid to get money. Now I want you three super stupid ass niggas to go all through the projects and let it be known that I don't want to hear another mu' fuckin' firecracker until the fourth of July."

"O-Okay Tank." Tiny stuttered as him and Marcus helped Dolla up off the ground. "Damn man, he fucked you up." Tiny whispered to Dolla as he saw blood leaking from his head.

"Tone, chirp Mack and let him know what's up. Tell them to meet us back in the cut. Gary, chirp Steve or A.P. and tell them I said to get the fuck on business before I come holler at them." Tank said as they made their way back over to the cut.

Tank wasn't feeling the shit that just happened. He didn't like redundant shit, and he tried to avoid dumb ass people at all times, that's the reason why he had key soldiers, so that they could deal with the dumb shit and have shit right so that when he came through he wouldn't have to do shit but pick-up money and drop-off weight. But his key soldiers were slipping. No one was supposed to be playing with fireworks, especially niggas that were supposed to be getting money. And if niggas were playing with fireworks, then somebody was supposed to hit the chirps and alert the hood. But nobody hit the chirps, and Mack said he left Steve and A. P in charge, but those niggas still hadn't showed up to see what happened.

It was time for Tank to stand on his guys and let them know that they were getting too comfortable, so as Mack and the rest of his guys were walking up, he started snapping. He let them know that he was shutting the projects down for the next few days, and that none of them were to leave or do anything unless he approved it.

☙

"Damn nigga, what's taking you so long to open up the door?" Donta inquired.

"I can't find my fucking keys. I think I left'em in Los car." Tray said as he went through his pockets for the third time.

Donta looked down the block just in time to see Los turning the corner. "That nigga down the street. Chirp his phone and tell him to come back."

As Tray pulled his phone out of his pocket and began looking through it for Los's chirp number, he didn't pay attention to the bubble that was pulling up on him until it was too late.

Chop! Chop! Chop! Chop!

The A.R woke-up the night as Zed put it out the window and let it ride. The first few slugs ripped Tray's chest open and lifted him off his feet.

Chop! Chop! Chop!

While Zed was still letting the A.R go, X put the car in park and hopped out looking for Donta.

On the other side of the car, Donta had managed to dip low and pull out his .45 Luger, but not before a slug grazed his arm and knocked a chunk out of it. He saw the way that Tray got hit-up and knew that if he wasn't dead, he was close to it. And he felt that if him and Tray had to go, then he was going to take somebody with them. He was just waiting for the shooting to stop so that he could hop-up and give whoever was shooting what they were looking for.

X made his way over to the other side of the bubble and was waiting for Zed to stop shooting so that he could go give Donta a few slugs to make sure that he was dead.

As soon as Zed stopped shooting, Donta waited a split second before he raised up, but that split second costed him, because as soon as he raised up, the last thing he saw was a bright flash before X blew his brains out the back of his head.

Up the block and around the corner, Los had pulled over to roll-up a blunt. He had the white girl remix banging and was about to go get up with his girl until he heard something that sounded like gun shots going off. At first he didn't think anything of it until it didn't stop, so he turned his radio down to make sure that he wasn't tripping. But when he turned it down the shooting had stopped. Now he really thought he was tripping until he heard another shot that sounded like it came from around the corner where he had just dropped Tray and Donta off at.

Just as he was about to throw his car in drive and go see what was going on, a black van pulled up on the side of him with the side door open. When he saw Zep's face, he reached for the 9mm on his lap, but was a little too slow. Zep had already put the Mossberg in his face, and as soon as he saw Los reaching he squeezed, blowing half of his face off and knocking him into the passenger seat. Zep knew that Los was dead from the first blast, but pumped another slug in him just for the hell of it.

☙

"What's up?" Reggie asked as he answered his phone after looking at the caller I.D.

"You already know what's up, but where J at?" Zed inquired.

"He in the room with the kissing cousins."

"Aw shit, you called them hoes up for him?"

"Yeah, you know I had to bring the best out for dude."

"I already know, but let me holler at him real quick."

"Aight hold up." Reggie said before he got up and walked towards the back rooms. He was still at the spot with Mikey playing the game while Lil J was in one of the back rooms getting his grown man on with Brittney and Marquisha, two of the badest red bones out of Homewood, Illinois. Reggie named them the kissing cousins because they were some bisexual freaks that looked just alike, but weren't related. They both shared the same olive skinned complexion and had long beautiful hair. Brittney was 5' 4" tall, while Marquisha was 5' 5" tall. They both had some voluptuous asses, but Marquisha's was a little fatter.

Reggie had called them up and told them to come welcome his man home, so as soon as they got there, that's exactly what they did. They took turns knocking him down while knocking each other down at the same time.

When Reggie walked into the room, Lil J was hitting Marquisha from the back while she was bent over devouring Brittney's juices.

"What up Reggie?" You finally decided to come get some of this shit huh?" Lil J asked as he continued to pound Marquisha out.

"Hell hah, I just came in here to let you know that Zed wanna holler at you. Here, he on the phone." Reggie said as he handed Lil J the phone. "I'ma 'bout to go back out here and finish beating Mikey ass in this game."

"Aight, but you sho' you don't want none of this shit? Brittney a beast with the head."

"I already know, that's why I called her up." Reggie said as he walked out the door and closed it behind him.

Lil J pulled out of Marquisha and pulled the condom off before he put the phone to his ear and walked over to the bed and laid down. "What up jo? What's good?" he hollered through the phone.

"Them two bitches you over there doing yo thang with, they what's good?"

"Yeah they what's happening, but is everything else good?"

"Yeah, everything good. But we about to go lay low and chill until the morning."

"Don't' forget to – "

"J, I'm on top of my shit man." Zed said cutting Lil J off before he said too much over the phone.

"Aight, I'ma get up with ya'll in the morning so that we can go to the mall and hit the lot."

"Don't forget we gotta go holler at dude."

"I ain't gon' forget." Lil J said before he got off the phone and put his hand on the back of Brittney's head letting her know what time it was. She looked up at him and smiled before taking his bullet into her mouth and did what she do best, showing him once again, that she was the real super head and all the rest were impostors.

When Lil J exploded inside of her mouth, she sucked, swallowed and kept going until he pushed her off of him, letting her know that he couldn't take anymore.

As he laid back and tried to regain his composure, Brittney turned around and stuck her tongue inside of Marquisha's mouth, giving her a taste of what she just had.

☙

On the other side of Harvey by the Hud, Detective Bradly was talking to Officer Thomas as he watched the coroner load Donta and Tray's bodies into the meat wagon.

"You think this was a set-up?" Officer Thomas asked.

Officer Thomas was a young man that knew too much about the system and not enough about the streets. He was on the force for two years already and was still green. But Detective Bradly knew that he would become a good Detective one day if he ever took the time to learn the streets.

"The way these niggas got hit-up, I ain't sho' what I think this is, but that could be a possibility; either that or a hit."

Detective Bradly was a smooth cat that had been on the force for eight years. Him and his partner Jones came to the force around the same time. They both were from the hood and knew a lot about the streets, and that was what made them some damn good detectives.

"Who would want to have them hit?" Officer Thomas inquired.

"Shit, with the way they've been robbing mu'fuckas ain't no telling. But what the witnesses saying?"

"They ain't saying nothing really. They act like they don't know nothing. One lady said she saw an all black car, but she don't know what make or model."

"What they say about the dude down the block with half of his face blown off?"

"Nothing. All we got down there are people saying they heard shots, but ain't nobody seen nothing. So the only thing we got to go off of is a black car, and that could be anybody. So to tell you the truth, we ain't got shit. This is going to turn out to be another unsolved homicide."

"Get used to it, because this shit is common around here."

"Do you remember that John Leebo dude that caught that case out in Robbins back in 2005?"

"You talking about Lil J? Yeah, I remember; why?"

"We got a fax earlier today from the States Attorney's Office, they said that the Judge found him not guilty this afternoon."

"That was a triple murder. How the fuck did they find him not guilty when they had two eye witnesses?"

"The fax said that the witnesses didn't show-up."

"Yeah, well I should've known that was going to happened, seeing as who we're talking about. That nigga Lil J ain't no ordinary cat. I've been watching him ever since him and his guy's were shorties; they some smart lil' dudes, always on top off their shit. I almost had their ass back in 2005 before Lil J got locked-up though. Him and his guy's had got too comfortable and started making mistakes, and I knew that it was only a matter of time before they did something stupid, and I was gone be right there to lock they asses up.

"But before it could happen, Lil J got locked-up and his guys tightened back up. But since you telling me he's back on the streets again, I'll be waiting on him. I wonder if he's back over there at the Vail Apartments."

"I had that beat over there around Vail a few times, they over there moving a lot of drugs."

"Hell yeah they are, and they smart with it too. They keep the peace in the area so that their spot won't be hot. Me and my partner Jones go through there every chance we get, but we don't ever see anybody but the workers, and they just pawns, so we let them do them until we need them."

"Speaking of Jones, where is he right now? I usually see you guys together."

"He's down there checking out the dude with half of his shit gone. He should've been on his way down here by now. Let me go down there and pick him up." Detective Bradly said as he walked off towards his car. "Ay Thomas?"

"Yeah."

"Loosen-up man, save all that proper shit for the station." Detective Bradly said before hopping in his car and pulling off.

CHAPTER 7

The next morning Lil J woke up out of his sleep and saw that he was so messed-up the night before that he had fallen asleep in the room with Brittney and Marquisha.

Man, I must've been outta there last night. I wouldn'a never fell asleep in here with these hoes, Lil J thought as he tried to get up but was stopped by Brittney. She had reached out and grabbed his sword. He knew exactly what she wanted so he climbed on top of her. "Girl, yo ass a freak." He said as he slid inside of her and began taking long deep strokes.

"Unnh……Unnh…..Unnh.." Brittney moaned waking Marquisha up.

Lil J was getting turned on from the way that she was moaning, so he pulled her legs up into the air and started banging her brains out.

"Unh……Unh…..Unh….Unh" she moaned as Lil J continued to pound her out until he exploded inside of her.

Damn, why the fuck I do that? He thought to hisself, knowing that he should have never busted inside of her. But it was too late now, so he just pulled out of her and threw on his boxers before grabbing his guns and leaving the room.

After he checked the apartment and saw that Mikey and Reggie were M.I.A, he hit the shower. He knew that they wouldn't have gone too far without waking him up; so he wasn't tripping.

When he came out of the shower, he saw that his whole crew was in the living room.

"It's about time you came up out of there." K.B said as he got up to greet Lil J.

"K.B what's up baby?" Lil J asked as he grabbed K.B into a bear hug.

"You already know what's up, a mu' fucka glad you home."

"Yeah man, I missed the shit out of you niggas while I was gone. Zep, nigga get up and show me some love before I fuck you up." Lil J said as he grabbed Zep by his hand and pulled him to his feet before he bear hugged him just like he did K.B. "What you been up to Lil bruh?"

"You know, the same shit. Just was trying to be easy until you came home."

"But now that I'm home you ready to act a damn fool ain't you?"

"You already know." Zep said with a slight smirk on his face.

"Ay shorty and them still back there?" Lil J asked referring to Brittney and Marquisha.

"Nah they gone." said Mikey

"Good. What's up with them stick-up niggas?"

"They memories." said Zed.

"Yeah?"

"Hell yeah, you know how we get down." said X. "But what's up? Is you ready to hit the lot or what?"

"Yeah, who all going with us?"

"Mikey and Reggie gone ride with ya'll." said Zed. "I'ma chill here and hold the block down. And while ya'll gone I'ma send Zep and K.B out to get a location on Rick."

"Aight that's what's up cause as soon as we get back I wanna go holler at dude."

☙

Three and a half hours after Lil J left the block, he was pulling back up in a pearl white 645 BMW with peanut butter guts.

Zed was sitting on the stairs talking to J.J and Ant when he saw the 645 pull up and park. He didn't recognize the car so he put his hand on his Glock and was ready to pull it until he saw that it was Lil J and Mikey.

"Ay Zed, you see my shit? Now tell me I ain't about to be shitting on niggas when I go to the sounds and rims shop and hook this bitch up." Lil J said as he hopped out of the coupe.

"Yeah, this mu' fucka right." Zed said after he came down the stairs and admired the exterior of the car. "Where X and Reggie at?"

"There they go right there." J.J said as he saw X's truck coming up the block.

"Let me see the keys J. I'ma 'bout to hit a block and see how she ride."

"Bruh, don't fall in love with my shit." Lil J said as he tossed Zed the keys.

"It's like that huh?"

"You a see." Lil J said as he watched Zed hop in his whip and pull off.

When Zed pulled back up he was all smiles. "Man bruh that mu'fucka the business. Make me wanna go trade in my Infiniti." Zed said as he hopped out of the car and tossed the keys back to Lil J. "But look, I just got a call from Zep. He say they got a location on dude."

"Where he at?" Mikey asked.

"He at the car wash on 159th Street with a few of his guys."

"Aight hold up." Lil J said. "Ay J. J, check it out. I want you and Ant to go up to the spot where the burners at and grab a pump and two choppers. Bring 'em down to X truck for me."

"Aight, we a be right back." J. J said as him and Ant dipped off.

"Yo Zed, they know how to handle them choppers?"

"Hell yeah, they gone get it in there if it go down."

"Aight. Ay X, they gone ride with you and Reggie. Reggie I want you to handle the pump.

"I got you." Said Reggie.

"I'ma need ya'll to be on business when we get over here because we might have to get it cracking." Lil J said as J. J and Ant came down the stairs with a Mossberg and two SK's.

Ten minutes later, Lil J and his guys were pulling into the car wash. It was packed with fine ass women and balling ass niggas riding in Benzes, Beemers, Lexuses, Lac's, and a lot of other fly whips. Guys were getting their cars washed and detailed, while others were just up there stunting.

Rick was leaning on his all black S550 talking to a few of his goons when he saw the Beemer, the Lac Truck and the Infiniti pull in. He didn't think anything of it at first until he saw Lil J and his guys hopping out of the whips with burners. Him and his guys were strapped and ready for whatever, but he really didn't want anything to go down at his place of business.

"Yo Rick, whats up with these niggas?" One of his goons asked as he pulled out his .357.

"I don't know, but be easy. I don't want shit to happen up here." Rick said as Lil J and Zed approached him. "What's up Lil J? What brings you niggas up here? And what's up with the heat?"

"You know why the fuck we here, and aw yeah, you ain't gotta worry about paying them stick up niggas off. I took care of 'em for you already. I know you sent them niggas at me."

"Hell yeah I sent 'em at you. What you thought I was gone deny it?" Rick asked matching Lil J's stare.

"Nah I ain't think that. But we need to get an understanding about this bullshit before it go too far."

"Go too far! Nigga it's already there. I know you ain't think you was just gon' change my brother and get away with it. And don't think that you or yo guys was the mu'fuckas that scared them witnesses into not coming to court on you. That was my doing so that we could handle this shit in the streets. So fuck getting an understanding. I want mines in blood." Rick said, letting his emotions get the best of him. He was talking too much and doing everything that his Uncles told him not to do.

I knew it was something else to them witnesses. Lil J thought. "I ain't no bitch cuz, so all that hot shit you hollering right now irrelevant, because me and my niggas came prepared to do whatever. So if we ain't gon' shoot it out and get this shit over with right now, then we need to get an understanding because the shit that happened wasn't my fault."

"What yo mean it wasn't yo fault?"

"I ain't know that was yo brother, and them cats brought that shit on they self. They was out there wilding and shit so I did what you or any other nigga woulda did in that situation. But look, I really ain't come through here to shoot bullshit back and forth with you. And the way I see it, what's done is done. We can't change what happened." Lil J said as he paused and glanced over to Zed who was clutching two chrome .45s "Now you can keep sending hits, and me and my niggas can start coming through shooting shit up until we all dead, or we can be playa's and get an understanding."

"So you just expect me to look pass what you did to my brother?"

"I ain't saying that, but like I said before, what's done is done. And it ain't like I just went over there to get down on him, the shit just happened."

Rick was getting tired of talking. He wanted to pull out his .44 mag and knock Lil J's brains out of his head. But he knew that would result into a big shoot out, and he didn't need that, especially at his car wash. "Right now ain't the time or the place to get an understanding. So I'ma have to get up with you later about that."

"Aight, but I'm telling you now. Call off the hits, because if somebody else come at me, you better hope they hit, cause if they miss, you gon' have some serious problems."

"Is that a threat?"

"Nah…..it's a promise!" Lil J said as him and his guys hopped back in their whips and pulled off.

"What's up Rick? What you wanna do about them clowns?" Wayne inquired.

"Fuck them niggas, they gone get what's coming to 'em!" Rick vented.

I knew we shouldn't have fucked with them goofy ass stick up niggas." said Calvin.

Calvin and Wayne were two of Rick's most trusted men. He looked at them like brothers ever since they grew up together back in the late 80s and early 90s before he went to jail.

"Fuck that shit, don't worry about it. Just find some better hitters that ain't from the hood, and make sho' they know what they doing."

"I'ma get right on top of that. I got a few niggas from Chicago Heights that's just right for the job. But what's up with the Fathers Day Picnic tomorrow?" said Wayne.

"You know, the same shit just make sho' that the security a lil tighter."

"I'ma 'bout to go back to the Village. I'll get back up with ya'll later." Calvin said before he got in his car and pulled off.

Rick stood deep in thought focusing on an old school that some older cat was wiping down. He was trying to figure out why the guy hadn't left with the rest of the people that broke out when they saw Lil J and his guys pull up.

"Yo Rick, here come yo crazy ass girl." Wayne said bringing Rick back from his thoughts.

"Aw shit." Rick said as he watched Dollicia pull up and hop out of her candy apple red L.S. 460.

"I'ma 'bout to go in here and check on these niggas. I'll be back." Wayne said as he dipped off.

"What's up baby?" Rick inquired as Dollicia walked up to him and put her arms around his neck.

"Nothing, I just came up here to see if you were ready to go shopping with me." Dollicia said after she kissed Rick in the mouth.

Dollicia was Rick's main chick. She was a beautiful honey complexion bisexual that had some nice ripe breasts, and an ass that drew attention from niggas and bitches.

Rick met her at the nail shop out in Markham two years ago. He was getting a manicure, while she was finishing up getting a pedicure, and was about to leave until he got up and approached her. "Excuse me Miss, I don't mean to bother you, but I wouldn't be able to forgive myself if I let you walk out of this nail shop without speaking to you."

Ooh shit. Who is this handsome nigga? Dollicia thought to herself as she admired Rick's bald head, and handsome face. "And why is that?" she inquired.

"Because I would feel like I missed a chance of a life time." Rick said as he smiled showing her his perfect set of pearly whites. "My name is Rick, and I would appreciate it if you gave me a call sometime." he said as he handed her a business card with his number on it.

"I'm Dollicia and I don't mean to be rude, but I'm kinda in a hurry so I'll think about giving you a call." she said as she grabbed the card and left.

"Rick never received a call from her and the next time he saw her was three months later at his club out in South Holland, Illinois. He was in his back office with Tank, Tone, Calvin and Wayne discussing the incident that happened to his little brother out in Robbins, when all of a sudden he looked at the monitor on the wall and saw her and another woman coming through his front door.

"So you want us to fall back?" Tank asked but his words fell on deaf ears because Rick was deep in thought thinking about how beautiful Dollicia was when he first saw her.

"Rick." Tank hollered bringing Rick back from his thoughts.

"What up?" Rick inquired.

"You telling us to fall back or what?"

"Yeah, but look, I gotta go take care of something real quick so we a finish this shit later." Rick said as he got up and went and found Dollicia at the bar with her friend.

"Put whatever these beautiful ladies drinking on the house." He said as he walked up and stood behind Dollicia. When she turned around to protest, a smile spread across her face when she saw who the Cartier Sport smelling brother was. "What's up beautiful? I was wondering when you was gon' call or come see me."

"And what makes you think I'm here to see you?" she asked still smiling. She was feeling Rick. He was handsome, and he had money, but she had been feeling him ever since he approached her at the nail shop before she knew he had money. She just didn't like jumping into relationships without first knowing who she was dealing with. She learned that lesson seven years back from her ex-boyfriend. He was a handsome nigga from the Southside of Chicago that had promised her the world when she first met him. She was young and callow, so she fell head over heels for him, and gave in to his promises.

Two weeks later everything changed. She found out that he was very possessive, controlling and insecure. He started beating her and threatened to kill her if she left him. She tried calling the police, but that didn't work. So one night when he came home fighting and accusing her of lying and cheating, she grabbed a butcher's knife and stabbed him thirty two times until he was unconscious. He later died at the hospital while she was at the police station being charged.

After she sat in the county jail for 13 months, the States Attorney dropped the charge down to second degree murder and she copped out. Three years later she received a pardon from the Governor and was released. Ever since then she vowed to herself that she would never jump into a relationship with her eyes closed.

"So what you telling me – you not?" Rick responded.

Dollicia looked deep into Rick's eyes debating on whether or not she should give him a chance.

"What is it that you want from me?" she asked, as her smile faded.

I wanna fuck yo brains out. Rick wanted to say, but didn't want to let the hood come out just yet, so he played the conservative roll, "Felicity."

A smile crept back across her face as she decided to let her guard down.

"This is my friend Meagan. Meagan, this is Rick, the guy I was telling you about.

"Nice to meet you Meagan." Rick said while extending his hand.

Meagan didn't respond, she just shook Rick's hand and gave him a seductive smile.

Dollicia, if you and yo friend wanna come over to the VIP section, ya'll more than welcome."

"Nah, we don't plan on staying. But if you still wanna get to know me, then give me a call." Dollicia said as she handed him a piece of paper with her phone number on it before she got up to leave.

Rick called her later on that night, then took her out to breakfast the next morning where she opened up and accepted him into her life. As the months passed and their relationship grew, he couldn't stand the thought of them being apart, so he moved her into his eight hundred thousand dollar crib out in Dynasty Lakes in Hazel Crest.

Two months later, he came home and caught her cheating in his bedroom. It was a Saturday night, and one of his clubs was jumping, so he called her and told her that he probably wasn't going to make it in until around five in the morning and asked her if she wanted to come out and kick it with him but she declined. So he went on and did him until 2 a.m. when he caught a massive headache that soured up his night. He was a little tipsy from sipping on some Hennessy, but he really wasn't feeling the night anymore, so he got up with is driver Dog and told him that he was ready to bounce after he let Calvin and Wayne know that he was leaving.

When he arrived at his crib and walked through the door, he heard slow music coming from upstairs. He thought that maybe his girl had fallen asleep with the radio on, so he waved his driver off before he closed the door. As he made his way through the house, he heard the sound of someone moaning coming from the upstairs.

Aw hell nah, I gotta be tripping. I know this bitch ain't got no other niggas in ma house, he thought to hisself as he became enraged and pulled out his .357 He couldn't think straight because the only thing on his mind was killing Dollicia, and whatever nigga she was fucking in his crib. He just couldn't fathom why she would betray him like this after everything that he had done for her.

As he made his way up the stairs, the moaning became clearer to him. It was Dollicia and she was moaning harder than he had ever heard her moan before and that only added fuel to the fire.

When he made it to the stairs he saw that his bedroom door was open, so he crept over to the side of it and looked in expecting to see the worst, but what he saw straight blew his mind. Dollicia was laid back in the bed still moaning while another woman's face was buried between her legs.

What the fuck! Her freaky ass been holding out on me, he thought as his anger turned into lust.

"So baby, this how we getting down on each other now?" Rick asked scaring the hell out of Dollicia as he walked into the room.

Meagan. I should've known that something was going on between these hoes, he thought after Meagan pulled her head from between Dollicia's legs.

"Baby please. I-I'm sorry. I b-been meaning to tell you." Dollicia stuttered as she slowly moved to the other side of the bed.

Rick sensed that she had become afraid and didn't know why until he realized that he still had his gun in his hand. "Aw don't mind me, I ain't tripping." He said as he sat his gun down on the night stand and started taking off his clothes. "The only thing I'm mad about is that ya'll started without me."

When Rick was fully undressed, Meagan walked up to him and sat him down on the bed before she dropped to her knees and started stroking his erect penis before taking him into her mouth. She had been wanting a piece of him ever since Dollicia introduced them at the club.

When Meagan started sucking on Rick's dick, Dollicia became jealous until she realized that this was what she wanted in the first place. So as Meagan continued doing her thing, she crawled over and began kissing Rick on the mouth before she laid him down and straddled his face.

It can't get no better than this, Rick thought as he began feasting on Dollicia's pussy.

Rick had his way that night and every night after that.

"Why the fuck won't you just get Meagan to go with you?" Rick asked responding to Dollicia's question.

"Because I want you to go with me. And why the hell is you catching an attitude with me? I ain't did shit to you."

"Damn baby, my fault. I'm still vibing off some other shit right now."

"What happened bae? What's wrong?"

"Nothing, don't worry about it. What time you try'na go to the mall tho?"

"Whenever you ready."

"Aight, wait for me in yo car while I go holler at Wayne real quick."

"Okay." Dollicia said as she stole another kiss before she let Rick go and got back in her car.

"Yo Dog, we about to go to the mall, so you and face know what it is." Rick said letting Dog, his driver and face, his bodyguard know that it was time to roll.

CHAPTER 8

Rick was raised in Harvey by his grandmother Sharon and his uncles Ron and Derrick. Sharon had taken him in and got custody of him after his mother died in a car accident when he was only four. His father was shacking-up with some broad in Robbins that he had got pregnant at the time. He thought he was a pimp, and said that he didn't have time for kids.

Ron and Derrick were heavies in the hood, and had the south suburbs on lock with the heroin and cocaine. While Rick was growing up, they made sure that he had everything he needed, and gave him everything he wanted.

When Rick turned ten years old, he found out that he had a little brother on his father's side, his name was Bobby and he was four years younger than him. He rarely saw Bobby though because his father only brought him over every once in a while.

Two years later, Rick found out that his father was stabbed to death by one of his hoes. And the next time he saw Bobby was when he turned seventeen. The year was 1990 and his uncles had put him on and bought him a 1990 Chevy Caprice, so he thought he was the shit. He had a pocket full of money; a .380 that he got from a crack head that was low on money; and Calvin, Wayne and James, three loyal niggas that would ride with him to the fullest.

He used to go out to Robbins every weekend to pick-up Bobby and take him shopping. He treated Bobby the same way that his uncles treated him, and at the end of every weekend before he dropped Bobby off, he would make sure that he gave him enough money to last him through the week.

When Sharon caught wind of what Rick was doing in the streets, she disapproved of it. So one night when he came in from running the streets, she told him that she knew about all of the trouble that him and his friends had been causing in school and around the neighborhood, and she was going to send him to Job Corps if he didn't straighten up.

Rick really didn't want to sit and listen to another one of her lectures, but he wouldn't dare disrespect her, so he sat and waited until she was finished before he promised her that he would straighten up.

While he was in his room getting ready to go to sleep, Bobby called and told him that some niggas had jumped him and took his new Jordans and his starter jacket. So he got back dressed and grabbed his .380 before he left the house ablaze. When he made it out to Robbins, Bobby was sitting on the front porch holding a bad of ice to his nose.

"What the fuck happened?" Rick asked after he hopped out of his car and walked up to Bobby.

When Bobby took the bag of ice away from his face and Rick saw the damage, he knew that he was about to make somebody pay. Bobby had a black eye and it looked as if his nose was broken.

"I was coming from my friend's house when some niggas walked up to me and told me to give them my shoes and coat. I told them I wasn't giving them nothing and they jumped me and took my shit." said Bobby.

"You know where them niggas be at?"

"Yeah, they be hanging around the corner."

"Aight, get in the car and show me where." Rick said as they both hopped in his Chevy.

When they pulled up to the niggas block, Rick saw four niggas leaning on a Cutlass. He could see from a distance that one of the niggas had on his brother's coat. He couldn't see the shoes, but just seeing the coat was enough to give him the green light.

"That's them niggas right there?"

"Yeah, that's them."

"Aight." Rick said as he pulled up next to the Cutlass before hopping out with his .380 and making the niggas come up out of his brother's shit. He didn't want Bobby to have any more problems out in Robbins, so he gave the nigga that had on Bobby's starter jacket a few slugs just to make an example out of him.

The next morning while Rick was in school, the police came and arrested him; then later charged him with the murder of Marcus Lewis. He didn't even make it to the county jail though because his uncles bonded him out of the courthouse for $20,000, which was chump change to them.

Back on the streets, Rick continued to get money with his friends while fighting his case for two and a half years until he copped out for 16 years at 50%. A year after he was down, he called the crib and found out that the Feds had locked his uncles up and took everything they had. Six and a half years later Rick was back on the streets.

☙

After Lil J and his guys left the carwash, him and Mickey headed out to his mother's crib in Homewood, Illinois, while the rest of his crew went back to the hood. His mother stayed in a three bedroom house that he bought her back in 2003 when he was copping from Rick.

When they made it out to Homewood, Lil J saw that his mother wasn't home so he decided to go out to Thorton, Illinois, a small, low key suburb that many people over looked. And that's exactly the reason why he moved his baby momma Karina and their son Malik out there. Not many people knew that he had a family and he wanted to keep it that way.

Back in 2004 when he found out that Karina was pregnant, he became enraged. He didn't want to have any kids because he wasn't done with the streets. Slick had told him when he was a shorty that he shouldn't start a family until he was done with the streets because a man's family was his weakness, and he didn't want to have a weakness. After she refused to get an abortion, he told her that she could keep the baby under certain conditions and restrictions which she agreed to.

The only people that knew about his family other than his mamma was his crew, and that was because he needed somebody to look after them while he was locked-up.

After making sure that no one was following him, Lil J and Mikey pulled up to Karina's house and caught her at the mailbox. Her hair was undone and she still had on her house coat like she had just woke up.

"Damn baby, did I catch you at a bad time?" Lil J asked as he parked his car by the curb and hopped out.

Karina was walking back up the driveway, but when she heard the familiar voice she stopped and froze in her tracks. She wanted it to be who it sounded like so bad, but she knew that wasn't possible because that person was still locked-up. She had talked to him two days ago and he hadn't said anything about coming home. So as she turned around and saw that it was who she wanted it to be, she dropped the mail that was in her hands before she ran and jumped into his arms.

"Aaaaahhh." She screamed out with excitement. "Bae, why didn't you tell me that you were coming home? You could've at least called me and told me that you were on yo way."

Lil J never let Karina visit him or come to court because he didn't want to run the risk of someone finding out about her, so she never knew what was going on, and Lil J liked it that way.

"Let you know I was on my way! What you got a nigga over here or something?" Lil J asked as he looked over to Mikey who was leaning on the car.

"Nah stupid, you know I don't get down like that." Lil J gave her a dubious look. "But if you would've called me, I could've did my hair and put some clothes on."

Karina wasn't a dime piece, but she was a solid eight. And although she wasn't one of Lil J's best looking chicks, she damn sure could compete. But Lil J liked her because she had other qualities. She was real and sincere, and she wasn't inquisitive like most of his other hoes.

She was from Alsip, Illinois, but after she got pregnant and agreed to Lil J's conditions and restrictions, he moved her out to Thorton, away from all of her talkative ass friends. She was an ambitious RN that was striving to become a doctor, so she didn't have time for friends anyway.

"It's two in the afternoon, yo ass should've been had some clothes on." Lil J retorted.

"Boy, it's Saturday, and I ain't gotta work today. I was planning on staying in the house and resting."

"Where my son at?"

"He in the house watching cartoons."

"You think he gon' remember me?"

"He should, but if he don't remember yo face, he should remember yo voice."

Lil J didn't even respond to that, he just shook his head. When they made it into the house, Malik was sitting in front of the TV eating cereal and watching Spiderman.

"Malik, look who here to see you." Karina said as she walked over to her son.

When Malik turned around and Lil J saw his face, he was at a loss for words. Malik was a nine month old baby when Lil J went to jail, but now he was a little boy version of him.

"Ma – who is dat?" Malik asked after giving Lil J a flummoxed look.

"That's yo daddy."

"I thought my daddy said he was locked-up?"

"Stop saying that, I told you that he was out of –"

"Don't lie to my son." Lil J said cutting Karina off. He hated when parents taught their kids how to lie by lying to them, then turn around and whooped them when they lied. "I was locked-up, but I'm here now." Lil J looked at his son's still confused face and knew just what to say to make him remember him. "What's good my Lil Prince?"

Malik smiled, remembering exactly what to say. "Big faces."

"You talking 'bout these big faces?" Lil J asked as he walked over to Malik and pulled out a pocket full of money.

Malik moved closer to his mother.

"Y-You can buy me Spiderman toys with dem big faces?"

"I can buy you whatever you want with these. When you wanna go get'em?"

"Can we go get dem today?" Malik asked with excitement in his voice.

"Yeah, we can go get'em as soon as yo mama put some clothes on you."

Malik's smile weakened as he looked up to his Mother. "Ma, you coming with us?"

Lil J sensed that he was still a stranger to his son, so as Karina gave him a look that asked if she was invited, he gave her a nod.

"Yeah, I'm going. Now come on and let's go wash up and get dressed." Karina said as she became excited. She was happy that Lil J had invited her and she wanted to hurry up before he changed his mind.

After Lil J watched Karina and his son disappear to the back of the house, he got up to go let Mikey know what was up. When he got outside, he saw Mikey talking to some fine ass woman walking a dog.

"Baby, I'ma get up with you later, just hit that number when you ready to kick it with a real nigga." Mikey said to the woman as he saw Lil J walking up to him. "What up bruh? You ready to ride?"

"Nah, I'ma chill here for awhile and take my son to the mall out in Indiana."

"Which one?" Mikey asked, as he glanced at an '72 Fleetwood that was coming up the block.

"The one on Grant Street." Lil J said as he handed Mikey the keys to his coupe. "I'ma chill out here for the rest of the night tho; so just come pick me up in the morning so we can slide through the Father's Day picnic."

"Aight, I got you." Mikey said as him and Lil J embraced before he hopped in the 645 and pulled off.

CHAPTER 9

The Father's Day picnic that took place at Cooper Park every year was a festival that everybody throughout the 100s and the south suburbs made sure to attend. The weather was 95 degrees, so most people predicted that this was going to be one of the best picnics.

By the time Lil J and his guys pulled up to the park, it was already jumping. Everybody from everywhere was there. From the playa's that was balling, to the clowns that was broke, and from the honey's that was bad to the bitches that was smoked.

Most of the guys were around the basketball court hooping or watching the game. While the ladies were either trying to snatch up a baller or just trying to be seen.

The kids were having fun in the park while everybody else was either cooking or eating.

"Yo Mikey, it's a lot of bitches out here today." Lil J said as he hopped out of his 645. He was rocking an Artful Dodgers fit with some all black Pradas, while the rest of his guys were rocking Red Monkey and Evisu.

"It be like this every year nigga, quit acting like you forgot."

"Shit, I almost did, but seeing all of these thick ass hoes out here today starting to bring back memories."

"I live for these picnics." Reggie said as they started walking towards the basketball court. "Look at all of these half naked hoes. In a few more years these bitches gon' be out here in G strings."

"Don't let these hoes make ya'll forget about the snakes that's out and about." Said Zed.

"Right, we wouldn't wanna get caught slipping now would we?" Lil J said as he looked around at all of the niggas and bitches that was kicking it in the parking lot.

A lot of people in the hood didn't think that Lil J was going to come from under the three bodies that he was fighting. So as him and his guys made it to the basketball court, most of the niggas that knew him, or knew about him were shocked to see him, while others were just happy to see that another nigga had beat the system.

"Lil J, what up man? When you come home?" A cat named Smoke that Lil J used to cop CDs from asked as he walked up.

"What up Smoke? What it is?" Lil J asked as he avoided Smoke's question and extended his fist to show him some love.

"Shit man, mu' fuckas told me that you wasn't never coming home."

"Well you know that's how it is when mu' fuckas out here praying on the next nigga's down fall."

"I already know, but look, I got all of the new and exclusive shit if you tryna cop something."

Lil J smiled. "You still fucking with them CDs huh?"

"Yeah man, a nigga gotta eat. Here go my card."

"Aight Smoke, be easy." Lil J said as he took the card.

"Lil J, what's happening playa?" Cash asked as he walked up.

"Shit, you know, just out here getting a feel of the streets again. What's up with you tho? You still breaking dice games and shit?"

"Yeah, you know I stay on that, but I ain't gon' hold you up playa. I'll get up with you later." Cash saw Tameka and Aliana walking up and didn't wanna stick around for her to start acting crazy, so he decided to move around.

"Aight nigga, stay up." Lil J said as he turned his attention to the basket ball game.

"Yo J, check out that nigga Rick over there on the sideline." said Zed.

When Lil J looked, he saw that Rick was standing on the side of the court intently watching the game with his entourage behind him. "His team must be about to play one of them teams next."

"Nah, that's his team on the court in the black and blue." X spoke up.

"I thought his colors was always red and white?"

"He changed that shit when his brother got change over."

"So blue and – "

"Lil J, you been home since Friday and still haven't called me. What the hell wrong with you?" Tameka snapped as she walked up.

Damn! Lil J thought after he turned around and saw Tameka. He hadn't seen her in a whole year and she was just as fine as she was when he last saw her. She had her hair in micros and was rocking the hell out of a BeBe fit that was exposing damn near everything.

"I didn't know I was obligated." Lil J replied after nodding to Aliana.

"What?" Tameka asked with a confused look on her face.

Lil J sensed that she was about to make a scene and right now wasn't the time for that, so he quickly changed up his approach to the situation.

"Meka baby, don't trip on that lil shit because right now ain't the time. So just come slide down on me later." Lil J said before he turned his attention back to the game.

Tameka took a step forward and was about to protest, but thought better of it when K.B. stepped up and blocked her path. She never got along with him and knew that Lil J would probably let him fuck her up if she started wilding, so she decided to step after sucking her teeth and rolling her eyes at him.

Over on the basketball court, Rick was supposed to be coaching his team, but his mind was a million miles away. Earlier he had got a disturbing call from his uncle Ron and was trying to figure out who he was getting his information from because when he called him he told him that he had heard about what happened Friday and Saturday, and let him know not to make another move until after their next visit which was Monday.

Rick didn't like answering to his uncles because he was a king on the streets. But he was too smart to let that king shit go to his head because the empire that he was running was theirs, and he didn't want to fuck up his position by stepping out and doing his own thing.

When Wayne informed Rick that Lil J and his guys were pulling up, Rick told him to just keep an eye on them. He didn't plan on talking to Lil J until after he hollered at his uncles because he didn't want to do something stupid and piss them off. So as Lil J continued to mingle with the crowd, he just continued to watch his team get blown out while his mind was still roaming.

☙

When Lil J and his guys left the picnic, they headed over to the building on 159th in Lexington. The building was a three flat apartment building that had about 20 to 25 units inside of it. Lil J had been wanting to snatch the block up but never got around to it. But now that his guys had snatched it up, he wanted to see how they were running it.

"So Zed, these the lil niggas ya'll got holding this building down huh?" Lil J asked as him and his guys pulled up to the building and hopped out of their cars.

"You talking about these cats that's posted up out here?" Zed asked.

"Yeah."

"Yeah, but they just on security."

"If they on security, then where the niggas ya'll got moving the work at?"

Zed and Reggie gave each other dubious looks before Reggie spoke up. "Them niggas in the crack spot, but we got this block set-up just like the other one. The only difference is this block ain't making as much money."

"What it's doing over here?"

"About 15 to 20 racks a day."

"You think it could be doing more?"

"Yeah it could, but that's only if we get some better shit."

"We need that shit Rick got , don't we?"

"Hell yeah. The work dude got a have this bitch do'n double what it's do'n now. But why you ain't holla at him at the picnic?"

"Because it's his turn to come holla at me. I already came at him once at the carwash. So it'll be redundant for me to come at him again. But anyway, ya'll ain't been having no problems over here?"

"Nah, not really. We had a few problems when we first came over here, but ever since then shits been smooth." said Zed.

"Ay Lil J, that bitch Brittney just text my phone asking about you." Reggie said as he was checking his messages. "She want yo number, you want me to give it to her?"

"Hell nah! I ain't tryna fuck with shorty."

"She called me yesterday asking about you too. So whatever you did to them hoes must've been exclusive, because they thirsty for you." Reggie said as him and the rest of the crew started laughing.

"Come on now, knock that shit off. Ya'll know I just fucked them hoes and said fuck them hoes. But back to business. Do them niggas from Robbins know about this block?"

"More than likely they do. They fuck with Rick and you know he prolly telling them everything."

"We need to get rid of them bitch ass niggas like asap!" K.B snapped.

"Aight, we gon' take care of them niggas real soon so don't trip. But we gon' keep our eyes open and be easy for awhile because ya'll know them people gon' be on bullshit because what happened the other night."

"How long do you plan on holding off before we make a move?" Zed asked.

"We gon' wait about a week or two, but that's only if them niggas don't start acting crazy. Don't worry about that shit too much tho', cause I ain't. I'ma 'bout to try to find a new connect with some better shit."

"That's what's up J, but don't get too comfortable out here because shit different from how it used to be."

"Yeah Lil J, them niggas from Robbins don't be playing no games when they be coming through." Zep said not liking how Lil J was playing the situation like it wasn't serious.

"Man ya'll starting to blow me. Fuck them niggas, they ain't on shit. Matter fact, I'm done talking 'bout that shit. I'm ready to go hook my whip up; so I'll get up with ya'll later. Lets ride Mikey." Lil J said as him and Mikey hopped in his coupe and pulled off. "Yo Mikey! What's up with them niggas? Why they tripping like that?"

"They ain't the ones tripping Lil J. You don't see things like we do. Right after you got locked up back in '05, them niggas from Robbins started coming through on bullshit. They was shooting shit up like every day. We lost a couple a workers and a lot of money behind that shit. Zed sent Zep and K.B to scope out the old projects to see how we could go through there and get down on they ass, but before we could go through there, you told us to fall back. But now that you out, we feel like it's time for us to give them niggas they just due."

"Mike." Lil J said as he grabbed his soulja slim. "Give it to 'em raw CD and put it in the radio. Don't trip on that shit, them niggas gon' get it sooner then lat – "

♫ *From what I was told niggas say I' gon' hit No Limit like Pac hit Death Row and make some money out the asshole* ♫

CHAPTER 10

When Rick made it to the Fed joint out in Indiana the next morning, he couldn't help but wonder what his uncle was gone say when they were face to face. He still kind of feared his uncle Ron like a son feared his father. His uncle Derrick on the other hand was a whole different story because he was like his big brother. Both Ron and Derrick were upright, fearless and independent, but Ron had a low tolerance for ignorance, and he was hard on Rick because he knew his potential.

It was Ron's idea to put something up back in '95 before they got locked up so that Rick could take over and hold the streets down when he came home. Their lawyers had found out through some connects that the Feds had been watching them and were about to indict, so they paid their connect to hold down 50 bricks for them until their nephew came home.

When Rick came home back in 2002, Ron wanted to make sure that he was capable of holding things down before flooding him and putting him in position, so he sent one of his most trusted hitters out there to watch after him and see what he was on. After about 5 months of investigation, Ron learned that Rick was out there doing good.

Rick had jumped head first back into the drug game after seeing that his people were fucked up. His little brother was out in Robbins nickel and diming, his uncles were in the Fed joint doing 40 years, and when he went to get up with Wayne and Calvin in the Village, he saw that they were doing the same thing that his lil brother was doing in Robbins. So he grabbed the eight stacks that he had stashed at his grandmother's house and went to cop nine ounces of crack and a pound of weed.

After he got Wayne and Calvin back on his team, he had them slamming the work and weed with hopes of coming up, which they eventually did after months of nothing but grinding.

Rick went from copping nine ounces of crack and a pound of weed every two weeks to copping a key of crack and five pounds of weed every week.

He was keeping his hands clean by letting Wayne and Calvin handle the drugs and that's what let Ron know that he was ready. When Christmas came around and Rick came to the Fed joint with his grandmother, Ron pulled him to the side and dropped the bomb on him.

Ron told him about the thirty bricks of cocaine and the twenty bricks of heroin that his old connect was holding, and let him know that it was time for him to step up and become the man.

Rick accepted the offer and had been doing his thing ever since.

While Rick was sitting in the visiting area deep in thought, Ron walked up and took a seat. He didn't speak for a whole two minutes. He just starred at Rick with a killer mug that made him become uneasy.

"Unk – " Rick started, but stopped as his uncle shook his head.

"Rick, you a intelligent man, but I don't understand some of the things you do." Ron said as he paused. "Around the time of little Bobby's death, I sent someone out to investigate what happened because I knew how you felt about yo little brother. But through investigation it was learned that little Bobby was out there reckless, which he shouldn't have been. When I asked you back in 2003 why was Bobby still out in the projects when he should have been somewhere lay'n back counting money with you, you told me that he didn't want to leave his guys in the hood; and instead of you persuading him to leave, you left him out there to gang bang and lose his life."

"How the fuck was I supposed to know that he was gon' lose his life?" Rick snapped, not liking the way that his uncle was laying everything out on the table so smoothly like he didn't know that his brother's death was part of his fault.

Rick was supposed to have pulled his brother out of the projects a long time ago and let him run things while he sat back in the shadows. But he was trying to let Bobby leave the projects on his own instead of forcing him to leave.

"Calm down Rick. I'm not coming at you like this to piss you off or make you feel bad. I just want to help you see things a little clearer. My sources told me that Bobby was out there disrespecting a lot of people, and that he was plotting to rob that guy ya'll call Lil J. Now tell me Rick, why the hell would somebody that could've had millions of dollars want to go out and rob somebody?" Ron said as he waited for Rick to respond. After about a minute of silence he continued. "Rick the shit that happened last week could've cost you a lot, and I don't want you to lose your life or your freedom over something that's already done. Killing Lil J or getting killed isn't going to bring Bobby back. And all of the shit that you on out there is starting to draw a lot of unnecessary attention to you. Attention that you don't need. You're supposed to be a legitimate business man, not a gangsta, so tighten up your shit. Them niggas was never supposed to know who ordered that hit." Ron said as he watched Rick's facial expression change.

See, that's the shit I'm talking about. How the fuck he always knowing shit. He must got a mu' fucka watching me or something." Unk, I understand what you saying, and I appreciate the pull up, but I just can't let my brother's death go unanswered."

"I'm not telling you to let it go unanswered, I'm just telling you to be smart about it because you don't want to go down for solicitation of murder for hire." Ron said as he paused. He knew that his nephew was going to go out and avenge his brother's death no matter what he said to him, he just didn't want him to get hurt in the process. As the visit was nearing the end, he gave Rick a few more wise words of wisdom. "You got to be a scientist out there in them streets Rick. Remember to keep yo friends close, but keep yo enemies closer."

When Rick was leaving out of the Federal building, the only thing that kept running through his mind was what his uncle had said about keeping his friends close, and his enemies closer. He now saw the mistakes he was making, and a few of them were crucial enough to cost him his life.

He knew that Lil J and his guys were some killers, so he shouldn't have never put out a hit without first making sure that it couldn't be traced back to him.

He caught a blessing the other day when Lil J and his guys came up to his carwash, because they could've come up blasting. He had to hurry up and get rid of him because having an enemy like him wasn't a good thing.

Lil J was very dangerous, and Rick was planning on bringing him as close as possible so that he could keep an eye on him, but he had to stall all of the hits first, so as he hopped into his Audi A8 he called Tank.

☙

Back out in the old projects in Robbins, Tank was laid back smoking on a blunt, while a hood rat named Laquita was giving him some okay head that he wasn't enjoying. It wasn't the fact that she wasn't taking care of good business because she was; it was just that his mind was somewhere else on more important things like catching up with the nigga that changed his guys. He had been trying to catch up with him ever since Friday, but the shit that was going on in his hood had him on hold. He wanted to make sure that he had shit together in his hood first before he went out handling other shit. As he was laid back thinking about what he wanted to do next his thoughts were interrupted by the ringing of his phone.

"Ay pass me that." Tank said to Laquita.

Laquita took his dick out of her mouth and grabbed his phone off the table before passing it to him and taking his piece back into her mouth.

When Tank looked at the caller I.D. and saw Rick's number, he knew that it was either something wrong or time to do some business. "What up?" he answered.

"Meet me in the Village at 9 o'clock. We need to talk."

"Do I need to bring somebody with me?"

"That's up to you."

"Aight." Tank said as he got off the phone and focused back on Laquita. She was just another bust down in the hood that wasn't on shit. The only reason he fucked with her was because she had the bomb on the pussy, other than that, she was a rat. "Get up and turn around." He said as he put his blunt out and pulled out a Magnum and put it on.

After he bent Laquita over, he entered her tightness loving the way that her pussy gripped his dick as he slid inside of her. He started taking long, slow strokes at first until her pussy was nice and wet, then he began pounding her out taking short strokes.

"Ooh shit….right there Tank." she said as she started throwing it back. "Unh…Unh…Ooh Tank….Don't stop….OH I'm cumin" she exclaimed as Tank continued to pound her out until he exploded.

"Damn girl…you just don't know." Tank said as he pulled out of her and fell back on the couch. Laquita fell back on the couch with him and as they both were sitting back trying to regain their composure, she broke the silence.

"Tank, I need some money to get my hair and nails done."

"Damn, didn't I just give yo ass some money the other day?"

"Yeah, but I bought my kids some clothes and shoes with it, and now I'm broke."

"Yo ass stay broke don't you?"

"It's these bills and these damn kids."

"Dude and them still ain't hitting you off to help you with them?"

"Hell naw, them broke ass niggas always act like they ain't got no money."

"That's fucked up. Go get a towel and get this shit off me so I can get up outta here."

"Alright, but is you gone give me the money?"

"Yeah I got you, now hurry up and go do what I said." Tank said as he grabbed his blunt and lit it back up.

CHAPTER 11

Ring! Ring! Ring!
What the fuck. Lil J thought as he woke-up and looked over to the cordless phone that was sitting on the night stand. After him and Mikey left the sounds and rim shop, he dropped Mikey off back in the hood before sliding over to his baby mama crib.
"K.L." Lil J said as he pulled the covers off of his baby mama.
"Hm." Karina moaned.
Ring! Ring! Ring!
"Get the phone."
"Why you ain't get it?" she asked as she reached over and grabbed the phone.
"Because it ain't for me." Lil J said as he got out of the bed and went to the bathroom. After he relieved hisself, he grabbed his toothbrush and hit his grill before hopping into the shower. Five minutes later Karina opened the shower door and stepped in.
"I know you ain't think you was gonna shower without me." Karina said as she reached around and grabbed Lil J's limp penis as she hugged him from behind.
"K.L. baby, yo freaky ass ain't get enough last night?" Lil J asked becoming aroused.
"Nope!" she said as she began stroking his erection. "I gotta get as much of this as I can because you know how you be dipping in and out on me."
Lil J was fully aroused now and had one thing and one thing only on his mind, and that was getting another nut off. So as he put down his soap

and towel, he turned around and pinned Karina to the wall before lifting her up and sliding inside of her.

Thirty minutes after wet sex and washing up, Lil J and Karina were hopping out of the shower drying off. After Lil J finished lotioning up and getting dressed he went and found his son in the living room sitting in front of the TV eating junk food.

"What's up lil man? What's happening?" he asked as he plopped down next to his son.

"Nuttin" washin' Spiderman."

"You love Spiderman don't you."

"Yeah, I wanna be Spiderman"

Lil J laughed as the commercials ended and Spiderman came back on.

"Dare he go white dare daddy!" Malik said with excitement in his voice."Dats me daddy!"

Lil J laughed again as his phone started vibrating. "I see you lil man." he said as he went on the front porch before answering his phone. "What up Reg?"

"What's good wit you bruh?"

"Shit, I'm laid back. What's good with you tho? You in the hood?"

"Yeah, I'm on the 9, but that nigga Rick just called my phone talking 'bout he need to holler at you. He want you to come through the Village later on."

"That nigga must be out his fucking mind. Call him – " Lil J paused as he thought about what he wanted to do. "Give me that nigga number. I'ma hit him up real quick."

"Aight, but hit me back and let me know what's up" Reggie said before he gave Lil J the number and hung up.

After Lil J dialed Rick's number, he answered on the first ring.

"Yo."

"This Lil J, what's happening?"

"I told yo boy to tell you to meet me in the Village in a couple of hours."

"Come on man, what the fuck you think I'm stupid?" Lil J inquired as he thought about how much of a death trap the Village was. It only had one way in and one way out. So if you rode through there on bullshit and wasn't a hundred deep or the police, you wouldn't make it out alive.

"What you mean?" Rick inquired.

"You can play dumb if you want to man, but if you wanna holler at me you can meet me on Vail around three." Lil J said as he ended the call.

Clown ass nigga, must think I'ma goofy. Lil J thought as he watched Zed pull up across the street and almost hit a old man in a cadillac that was driving past.

"My bad old timer." Zed hollered out the window as he parked his car.

"Zed, you better drive right out here man, these white folks a lock yo ass up out here." Lil J said as Zed hopped out of his car and walked up to him.

"Fuck these people. What's good with you tho?"

"Shit. I just got off the phone with that clown ass nigga Rick."

"What he talking about?"

"He wanted me to meet him in the Vill later on."

"What you tell him?"

"Fuck you think I told him? Hell nah. I let his ass know that if he wanna holler at me he can meet me on the block around three."

"You think he try'na pull a stunt?"

"I don't know, but we a know if he don't show up."

"I'ma have shorty and them posted with them choppers just in case."

"Aight that's what's happening, but what you on anyway? I see you in the Chevy."

"Fuck the Chevy. Mikey told me that you did yo thang with the Coupe."

"Yeah, I banged that bitch out like I said I was, and threw some 22" Asanti's on that mu'fucka. I got it in the garage, you wanna see it?"

"Nah, I'll check it out later. I got a call from Slim early this morning tho, he say he gotta few problems out west and need me and Zep to come out there for a few days."

"When he want ya'll to come out there?"

"Shit, he say asap, but I told him that I'ma have to get back with him because of the shit that we got going on out here."

"Aight, wait until we see what this nigga Rick on, then ya'll gone head and shoot out there."

"What time you plan on hitting the block?"

Lil J looked at his watch and saw that it was twelve forty. "I'll be out there in about an hour and a half."

"Aight, I'm 'bout to go get my hair braided. I'll be there when you get there."

Two hours later, when Lil J pulled up on Vail and was getting out of his car, he saw Ant posted up on the balcony and knew that he was holding something serious.

"Yo Ant, what you working with?" Lil J asked as he tucked his two .45s in each one of his back pockets.

Ant stood up and showed him a AR-15. "Zed and them upstairs in the last apartment waiting on you."

"Hit them niggas up and let 'em know that I'm out here."

"I already did."

"Aight." Lil J said as he walked to the middle of the building where J.J and K.B were posted smoking a blunt. "What's up?" What you niggas on?" Lil J asked as they greeted each other.

"Shit, just blowing a lil kush and kicking bullshit back and forth." K.B replied.

"J. J, them niggas from Robbins came back through here yet?"

"Nah, I ain't seen them niggas since Friday."

"Keep the guys on point cause them niggas might be on some snake shit. Matter fact, did Zed let ya'll know what the business was?"

"Yeah, he say that nigga Rick suppose to be coming through, right?" K.B asked.

"Yeah, he say he wanna holla at me, but I don't trust him, so I want security tight."

"I already got it tight." J. J said as he looked over to the balcony where Ant was posted.

"I got Ant posted up there watching the front, and I got Brandon doing the same in the back. I got B and Mal posted on each end of the balcony over at them buildings too." J. J said as he nodded towards the complex next door.

"Ay Lil J, there go Tameka stanking ass." K. B said as he watched Tameka pull up and park her Monte Carlo.

"Shorty was riding through here all night looking for you too." said J. J.

"I already know." Lil J said as Tameka walked up snapping.

"Lil J why da hell you have me coming through here yesterday knowing damn well you wasn't gonna be here?"

Trick ass bitch. K.B thought as he watched Lil J walk Tameka back towards her car.

"I had to take care of some business yesterday and forgot."

"So why ain't you call me when you remembered?"

"Shit, I ain't got yo number."

"My number the same Lil J. It ain't never change."

"Why you stop answering my calls while I was – " Lil J paused. He really didn't want to go back and forth with her about some bullshit that he really didn't care about, because he really didn't care about her. In fact, the only reason that he use to fuck with her in the first place was because she was a bad bitch. And he was known for sliding through the hood with bad bitches. But now that the niggas in the hood had their way with her, he felt like he had to play her with a string longer than the one that he use to play her with. "You know what? Fuck that shit, I'm here now. What's up?"

Tameka smacked her lips and leaned on her car. "What you mean what's up?"

"I mean, what' good? How you feeling?"

"You know how I'm feeling. You been playing me shitty for the last few days."

"I just been busy. It's a lot of shit that I gotta get caught up on. I been gone for two years."

"So am I gonna be able to see you tonight?"

"I don't know. I gotta see." Lil J said as he thought about the lil chick that he bumped at the sounds and rims shop.

"See, that's the bullshit I'm talking about. When the hell is you gonna have some time for me?"

"I just said I'ma see. Now quit acting stupid."

"What's yo new number? Tameka asked as she pulled her phone off of her clip.

Lil J really didn't want to give her his number, but he knew that he wouldn't be able to get rid of her if he didn't, so he gave it to her.

"Bay, I missed you, and I'm sorry for – "

"Don't worry about that shit Meka. We a have time to make up later, but right now I got some other shit to take care of." Lil J said cutting Tameka off. He didn't want to hear her bullshit, and he was tired of talking to her.

"Okay baby, I'ma call you. I love you." Tameka said as she opened her car door. She waited for Lil J to respond before she got in.

"I love you too."

When Lil J walked back over to where K. B and J. J were, he saw that Zed, Zep and X had come out.

"What's good with you niggas? Where Reggie and Mikey at?"

"Them niggas up stairs playing the game." said X.

"How much they playing for?"

"Five hundred a game."

"Mikey up there breaking Reggie ass ain't he?" Lil J asked as he turned around after hearing a car door slam.

"Hell yeah, he – "

"Damn! Who the fuck is that?" Lil J cut Zep off.

When Zep looked over and saw who Lil J was talking about, he shook his head. "That bitch stuck up. Her name Beautyful, tho."

"She thick as fuck. Ain't nobody cracking her?" Lil J asked as he watched Beautyful go up the stairs.

"Hell nah, bitch think she too good."

Shorty bad. I gotta get her. Lil J thought. "What's her real name?"

"Shit, I think that is her real name."

"J that bitch ain't going so don't even waste yo time. But look, here come dude." Said Zed.

Don't waste my time. Yeah right. "Chirp Mikey and Reggie and tell them to come out here." Lil J said as he watched Rick and Calvin hop out of a money green Audi. An Escalade was right behind the Audi so Lil J knew that it held his goons. "Zed, come with me. The rest of ya'll just be on point and watch them niggas in that Lac truck."

"What's up Lil J? How you feeling baby?" Rick asked as him and Calvin walked over to Lil J and Zed who was now posted on the side walk in front of the building.

"I'm good, but what's up tho?" What you wanna holler at me about?" Lil J asked not really caring for the bytalk.

Rick looked up at Ant posted on the balcony and knew that Lil J had him on security. He also knew that it was going to take some time to regain Lil J's trust, so he decided to cut to the chase and get right down to business.

"Check it out." Rick said as he walked a few feet away from Zed and Calvin. "I didn't come over here to shoot bullshit back and forth. I think we did enough of that at my carwash. But I been thinking about what you said about getting an understanding!"

Lil J nodded his head.

"Now I ain't gon' sit here and stunt like I ain't still fucked up about what happened to my brother. But I understand that sometimes shit happens, and getting an understanding about this shit a be better than strapping up and killing each other. So right now, I want to put everything in the past behind us, and get back to business."

"That's what's up." said Lil J. He knew that Rick was on some bullshit and didn't trust him. But he decided to go along with the bullshit just for the hell of it. "But I don't know about the getting back to business part. I mean when I got locked up back in '05, you raised the prices on my guys."

"Don't worry about the prices. Back to business means back to business." Rick said as he extended his hand. "Do we got an understanding?"

"What about them niggas from Robbins?"

"They on their own thang. I ain't got nothing to do with them."

"Aight." Lil J said as he shook Rick's hand. He knew damn well that Rick was lying but he didn't care because they all were going to get it sooner or later. "We gotta understanding."

✧

"I got $500 you don't straight 9, and another five you don't 9 or 5." Cash said as him and a few more heavies were shooting dice inside one of Rick's low key spots in the Village.

"Drop it nigga, you ain't said shit." Rick said as he dropped a thousand dollars on the floor and waited for Cash to drop his dough. "Aight nigga, I ain't got a 9 to 5, but I damn sho' fuck with them 9s." Rick said talking a little shit before he shook the dice and let'em go. "Damn!" he hollered as an eleven turned out.

"Bet back?" Cash asked as he picked up five hundred.

"Bet nigga." Rick said as he dropped another five and rolled the dice.

"Give me those." Cash hollered catching the dice. "Nigga put some shake on them bitches, my money don't lose that way."

"Fuck you nigga, just catch what you don't like." Rick said before he picked the dice back up, shook 'em, and let 'em go with a little bit of a spin to 'em. The first one that stopped landed on a four. The second one kept spinning until it stopped and landed on a three.

"Forty third nigga, give me my cake!" Cash hollered as he picked up his winnings after Rick crapped out.

"My dice, two I shoot. I need a fader not a friend." A chubby nigga named Shawn hollered as he picked up the dice.

"Two you shoot? You shoot'n two stacks" Cash asked with a avid look on his face. Shooting dice was his thing and he loved it when niggas raised the bar, but that wasn't what Shawn was trying to do.

"Hell nah, I'm talking about two hundred."

"We shooting fives or better, so put up another three with that shit or fall back." Kane, another one of the heavies hollered.

"Come on man, shoot my two."

"Fuck that, everybody else shooting fives, so put another three up and quit holding that shit to yo chest."

"I got him for the two, he my back man." Rick said dropping two hundred on the floor. As he watched Shawn shake the dice and let 'em go he felt a tap on his shoulder. "Give me those." He hollered catching the dice before he turned around and saw one of his soldiers named Snake.

"Ay Rick, Wayne sent me to tell you that Tank and his guys here to holler at you."

"Where they at?"

"Over in Forest Hills."

"What's up Rick?" You gon' watch this money or what?" Cash asked.

"Be easy Lil homie, can't you see I'm hollering?"

"I'm just saying man, a nigga try'na get this money and you holding us up.

"Here Snake, take this and break these niggas while I'm gone." Rick said as he gave Snake six stacks and left the spot.

Forest Hills consisted of two, two flat apartment buildings that sat on the north side of the Village.

When Rick got over to Forest Hills where Wayne and Calvin were at, he saw that Tank was there along with Tone, Mack and Rob.

"What's good Tank? What's happening with you?" Rick asked as him and Tank embraced.

"Shit man, I been try'na to catch up with this old bitch ass nigga."

"I see you got yo hitters with you."

"Yeah, you know how I get down. Neva know when I might have to get on some gangsta shit out here."

"I feel you, but lets step outside tho." Rick said, as he walked back out the door. "Tank, I called you over here because I need you to hold off on pushing on Lil J for awhile.

Tank frowned his face up "For what?"

"It's too hot right now and he on point. Somehow he knew about the hits that a nigga had out on him; and he also knew who was suppose to carry out the hits. That's how three niggas came up missing the other day."

"Damn, that was dude work?"

"Hell yeah. Him and his guys came to my carwash the next day with choppers and shit too. Talking 'bout we need to get an understanding."

"Why ain't you get rid of his ass that day?"

"Because it's too hot, and I ain't try'na do nothing stupid. I wanna get rid of his ass and still be on the streets. Not get rid of his ass and be somewhere doing a hundred years. But anyway, I need this shit to mellow back out. Them three niggas that got changed and that lil shit at the carwash then directed to much attention my way."

"How long you try'na get me to hold off?"

"I ain't sho', but just hold off for awhile."

"I'ma see what I can do, but I ain't making no promises."

"Aight, just do what you can."

CHAPTER 12

Two weeks had passed since Lil J got an understanding with Rick. And in those two weeks things had been going smooth for him and his guys. Their blocks were doing better, and the money was flowing in just like they expected.

The niggas from Robbins weren't coming through the hood on bullshit yet, but they knew that it was only a matter of time before Tank and his guys started coming through, so they stayed on point.

"Damn, that look like shorty car." Lil J said while pointing at the gas station. Him and K.B were riding east on 147th street coming from the DMV. They were inside of K.Bs 85 Chevy Caprice. It was painted the same color as a Pepsi pop with some Pelle leather guts, sitting on 28s.

Plies, a car full of choppers was banging and K. B couldn't hear a word Lil J was saying, so he cut the volume down. "What you say? " he asked.

"Turn around and go to that gas station back there."

"For what?"

"I think I just saw something."

"Aight." K. B said before turning around at the light. When he pulled into the gas station he had his Glock in his hand and was ready to get it cracking.

"What up Lil J? I thought you said you saw something up here?" he asked as he scoured the area.

"I did. Pull over there to that Grand Am."

"What?" K. B asked as he looked over to a blue Grand Am that was parked on the side of the station with the hood up. I know this nigga ain't have me turn around for no bitch.

"Pull on the side of that Grand Am."

"Lil J, you crazy man." K.B said as he did as he was told.

"What's up Baby Girl?" Lil J asked as they pulled on the side of Beautyful's car. She was sitting in the driver's seat looking hopeless and depressed.

"Hey." Beautyful retorted. Her car was acting up and she really didn't feel like being bothered because she was already ten minutes late for work.

Beautyful was a fine brown skin school girl that had a body that stopped traffic. She was known in the hood as the stuck up type, but the truth was she just didn't have time for a relationship, games, or bullshit because she was too busy working and going to school trying to build a foundation.

Lil J sat ogling at Beautyful for a whole two minutes before he spoke again. "Beautyful, what's wrong? Why you looking so down?"

Beautyful exhaled a deep breath. *Damn, can't you see that I don't wanna be bothered. Maybe if I ignore ya ass you a leave me alone.* She thought to herself before Lil J got out of the car that he was in and leaned against it. *Or maybe not.*

"What's wrong with the car?"

Beautyful remained silent.

Lil J knew that she was putting on a façade, so he continued to pry. "Baby Girl, I'll sit right here for however long it takes."

Persistent. "I just met you the other day Lil J. So you can stop calling me Baby Girl. And I would appreciate it if you would just leave me alone." she snapped.

She remembered my name, that's a plus. "I wouldn't be able to sleep right tonight if I left you out here stranded."

Beautyful chuckled. "You hardly even know me; so why would you care about me being stranded?"

"It ain't about me knowing you, it's about you being from my block. And everybody from my block is my family.

"Yeah, well I'ma big girl, I'll be alright."

Lil J gave her a dubious look. "What's wrong with the car?"

You just don't give up do you. "I don't know, but the guy that helped me push it out the street said that it might be my trans."

"Where was you on your way to?"

"Inquisitive aren't you?"

"Is it a crime?"

"Yeah."

"Stop it." Lil J said returning the sarcasm.

"I was on my way to work."

"You want us to drop you off?"

"Nah, I don't know ya'll that well. And besides, I already called a cab."

"What about the car?" You gon' leave it here or call a tow truck?"

"I'ma leave it here…shit, I barely got enough to pay for this cab."

"So how the hell you plan on getting it fixed?"

"I don't know, why? You gonna fix it for me?"

"You want me to?" Lil J asked as a car pulled up and blew the horn.

"Naw, I'm cool because I don't' want you thinking I owe you something. But there go my cab. I gotta go." Beautyful said as she started gathering her things.

She playing hard to get like a mu' fucka; but I gotta trick for her ass. "Aight Baby Girl. I'll see you later." Lil J said as he jumped back into the Chevy.

"You done playing mack daddy?" K. B asked as he threw his car in drive and pulled off.

"Fuck you nigga."

"Yeah. yeah. Where we headed tho'?"

"Swing through the hood real quick." Lil J said before he grabbed his phone and hollered through his chirp. "Yo, J. J."

"What up?" J. J chirped back.

"I need you to have somebody take care of something for me."

☙

Rick and Wayne were out in Dolton chilling in one of the back offices of Rick's bowling alley. They were drinking on some Ace of Spade and playing poker with Greg, P'nut and Dave; some getting money niggas from Chicago Heights that Wayne knew.

Wayne had started fucking with Greg back in the late 90s when Rick was locked up.

Greg and his guys used to come out to Harvey to cop happy sticks from Wayne back when he used to fuck with the water. They ended up getting real tight back when Wayne was about to get robbed one time when Greg came to cop from him.

It was the middle of the night when Greg called him and told him that he was coming through so Wayne told Greg to come to his house; something that he didn't usually do.

When Greg made it to the crib, Wayne was standing on the front porch talking on the phone so he got out of his car and approached him. Two minutes later three niggas dressed in all black emerged from the side of the house with guns drawn.

Wayne became furious thinking that Greg set him up, until he heard a car door slam drawing everyone's attention except Greg's away from the matter at hand.

Boom! Boom! Boom! Boom! Was all Wayne heard as he dove to the ground for cover. When he looked up he saw that Greg had taken out two of the robbers, and Dave, who had got out of the car, was still firing at the third one that was trying to flee.

"Greg, it's two reasons why I'm gon' need ya'll to be on business if I call ya'll up to take care of these niggas for me. The first reason is because I don't need this shit coming back to me. And the other reason is because if ya'll don't, then ya'll might turn up missing. And I don't need that because then I'm gon' lose out on all of that good money that ya'll making out there in the Hights." Rick said before he threw five $20 chips up in the Texas Hold'em poker game to start the bidding after the flop, which was an ace of clubs, a two of clubs and a king of diamonds.

"I bet." Greg said, before he threw up five 20 chips. "If you do decide to call us up, you ain't gon' have to worry about the shit coming back to you, and as far as us coming up missing, that shit is out of the question."

"Greg don't underestimate these niggas man."

"You saying that like dude and his guys some killas or something?"

"Greg, that's exactly what they is. I told you what they did to the last niggas that I sent at them."

"I bet that hundred and raise ya'll another hundred." Dave said as he threw his chips up.

"I call." said Wayne.

"I fold." said P'Nut.

"I call." said Rick.

"I fold." Greg said, before flipping over the next card, which turned out to be a two of hearts.

"I bet another hundred." Dave said throwing his chips up. It was already an ace of clubs, a two of clubs, a king of diamonds, and a two of hearts turned over. Dave had an ace of hearts, and a king of spades in his hand. He was hoping that the last card turned out to be either an ace, two, or a king so that he would have a full house.

"I fold. " said Wayne.

"I bet." said Rick.

Greg flipped the last card over and it turned out to be one of the cards that Dave was looking for, a king of clubs. Dave looked at Rick's face searching for a sign, but found none.

"I check." said Rick.

Dave smiled. "Naw naw boss. Ain't no free rides." He said as he grabbed his hundred dollar chips. I bet $500."

"I'ma call just for the hell of it." Rick said as he threw his chips up. "Now turn out and be a winner."

"I gotta boat nigga." Dave said laying down his kings over aces. "What you got a straight or a club flush?"

"Shit, I ain't even got that."

"Well, you know what it is." Dave said as he reached out and grabbed the chips.

"Naw naw Boss!" Rick said as he mimicked Dave before laying his cards out. "I gotta poker."

"Mutha fucka!" Dave hollered as he let the chips go and hopped out of his chair. "Ma' fucka beat me with four little ass duces!"

"Ay Rick, if these niggas some killas like you say they is, then me and my guys gon' need some time to scope them out before we come at them." said Greg.

"Aight, do ya'll because right now I get somebody else on them niggas." Rick said referring to Tank and his guys. He had been giving them the red light for about two weeks, and knew that they were getting impatient. "Just make sho' ya'll be careful."

☙

Tank, Rob, Mack and Tone were in the projects heated up posted in the cut drinking some Hennessy Privlidge, and smoking kush while they watched over the hood. Besides Lil J, they had other problems like the beef that they had with the niggas in the new projects.

Tank looked at the niggas in the new projects as more of a factor than he did Lil J because they were from the projects just like him. And he knew how niggas in the projects got down, but he wasn't underestimating Lil J though; because he had heard stories about him, plus he still remembered what happened to his guys back in '05.

Tank and his guys were standing about thirty strong or better in the old projects. And he begirded himself with nothing but the killas whenever he was in the hood or out in the streets on some gangsta shit. Right now he was chilling trying to figure out why Rick was still stalling on giving him the green light.

"Yo Tank, what's up with yo man cuz? This nigga been holding us up for damn near a month now. What's up with that?" Tone asked as he passed Rob another swisher to roll up.

"I don't know what's up with this nigga, but I'ma 'bout ready to say fuck waiting on him and do my thang." said Tank.

"You know what?" Mack spoke up after hitting the blunt that was already buring a few times before he passed it to Tank. "You woulda thought that Rick woulda been done gave us the word seeing as that it was his brother that got changed."

"Yeah, that's the same thing I was thinking, but the way that he stalling us out got me confused."

"What that nigga Wayne say when you called him earlier?" Rob asked as he started rolling the swisher that Tone passed him.

"He told me that he was gone holler at Rick and get back to me."

"Them niggas on some – "

"What the fuck!" Tank hollered, as he cut Tone off after seeing AP pull his banger from his waist and walk up on a dark colored Cutlass in the parking lot. "Ay ya'll go see what the fuck going on." He said before picking up a SKS. Tone also picked up a chopper and as the rest of the guys ran out to the parking lot, him and Tank stood on point making sure that nobody ran out of a cut on some snake shit.

Out in the parking lot, Rob, Mack and about fifteen more soldiers had the Cutlass begirded, while AP was checking the niggas out.

"Man, this look like Leroy car!" AP hollered to no one in particular.

"Ay, what's up jo! I ain't got no banger." The driver of the car stated as he took his hands off the steering wheel and raised them in the air just to let the niggas see that he wasn't on no bullshit.

"Man fuck that!" This look like Leroy shit!" AP hollered again.

"Leroy! Man who the fuck is Leroy?" the driver asked.

"Yeah cuz, this do look like Leroy shit." Lil Bill said nodding his head.

"Which Leroy? I got a cousin name Leroy." The passenger hollered back.

"Man who the fuck is Leroy? The driver asked as he looked from his man in the passenger seat, to the guys outside the car.

"Ay man, you don't know who Leroy is?" Mack walked up and asked the driver.

"He'll naw."

"Who car this is?"

"This my shit."

"And you don't know Leroy?"

"Nah."

"What the fuck you doing over here then?"

"I came to pick up a bitch."

"Pick that bitch up and ride out then." Said AP.

"Nah, pick that bitch up down the street." Rob said as him and Mack dipped back into the cut after watching the Cutlass pull off.

"What was that shit all about?" Tank asked as him and Tone came back into the cut.

"You know that nigga Leroy from the new projects right?" Rob asked as he laid down his Moss Berg.

"Yeah, what about him?"

"That was some niggas in a car that looked just like his shit."

"Was it?"

"Nah, that car was sitting up too high, and the rag was fucked up. But one of the niggas said that Leroy was his cousin."

"So why didn't ya'll get down on them niggas just to send a message then?" Tone asked.

"I don't know, but it probably was a good thing that we didn't because the driver didn't know what the hell was going on. And the passenger couldn't have possibly knew what was going on because if he did, then he wouldn't have said that Leroy was his cousin."

"What the fuck was they doing over here anyway?" Tank asked.

"They claim that they came to pick up a bitch, so we told them to pick the bitch up down the street."

೮

Out in Midlothian at the One Stop Insurance Agency Inc. Beautyful had just finished writing up her last quote for the day and was ready to go home. She looked at the clock and saw that it read 7:58 pm, exactly two minutes before she was to get off. She was hoping that her boss Mrs. Fannie came back from the bank next door within the next minute so that she could leave on time because she had to ride the bus home. Plus she still had to find out how she was going to get her car fixed.

Thank God, Beautyful thought as Mrs. Fannie walked through the door.

"Girl, I thought you said your car broke down on you and that you had to catch a cab?" Mrs. Fannie asked with an attitude.

"My car did break down on me. And I did have to catch a cab here." Beautyful replied with an addled look on her face.

"I know you ain't that damn stupid to park your car right in front of the building and come in here and lie to me?"

Beautyful got up and walked over to the door and was about to continue to protest until she saw her car parked by the curb. *How the hell*? She thought. "Mrs. Fannie, I don't even know how to explain this so I'll just see you in the morning." She said as she grabbed her things and walked out the door wondering how the hell her car got there.

When she opened the car door she noticed a steering wheel that she didn't recognize and was about to close the door back until she saw a note with her name on it laying on the seat. When she picked up the note she saw initials at the bottom that read L.J., but was still confused until she read it.

WHAT'S UP BABY GIRL. I KNOW YOU PROLLY WONDERING WHAT'S UP, SO I'MA JUST GIVE IT TO YOU STRAIGHT. I STOLE YO CAR AND GOT EVERYTHING FIXED BEFORE DROPPING IT OFF IN FRONT OF YO JOB. I KNOW YOU PROLLY FEEL LIKE YOU OWE ME RIGHT NOW SO I'LL TELL YOU WHAT. STOP BY THE PIZZA JOINT ON YO WAY HOME AND BRING ME A XL GROUND BEEF AND CHEESE PIZZA AND WE EVEN. MY NUMBER ON THE BACK IF YOU GOT ANY QUESTIONS.
P.S. THE KEYS TO THE IGNITION ARE IN THE ASHTRAY ALONG WITH THE MONEY FOR THE PIZZA.
LJ

This nigga crazy. Beautyful thought. When she opened the ashtray she saw a crispy one hundred dollar bill sitting underneath the keys. "This way more than enough for a pizza." She said to herself before she started the car and pulled off. "That boy crazy if he think I'ma 'bout to pick him up a pizza." She said but still found herself stopping at the pizza joint.

After twenty minutes of waiting on the pizza she was back on the road. When she made it to the block she saw that J. J and his pervert ass friends were posted. She didn't like them because they were always doing nasty shit, like pissing under the stairs, and spitting on every damn thing.

After she parked her car and was walking up the stairs with the pizza in her hands, she scanned the area for Lil J, but didn't see him so she kept it moving.

∽

"So Lil J, you just gonna walk out on me after I just got through sucking yo dick?" Tameka asked as she walked up on Lil J while he was zipping up his pants.

Two minutes ago Lil J was getting some okay head from Tameka and was really thinking about pounding her thick ass out until his phone started ringing. At first he disregarded it until he thought about who it might've been. And knowing who it might've been he didn't want to answer the phone in front of Tameka's hating ass, so he made up a good excuse to leave after he busted all in her mouth.

"I told yo ass I'll be back later, now be cool." Lil J said before he tucked his banger inside of his back pocket.

"Fuck coming back later. You can take care of me now and go do whatever you gotta do later."

"Nah, I'll be back."

"Fuck yo bitch ass, you ain't gotta come back!" Tameka hollered as she grabbed a cup off the dresser that had some red Hawaiian Punch in it and threw it at Lil J.

"What the fuck!" Lil J hollered as the juice splashed all over his white tee. "You dumb ass bitch."

"Fuck you! I hate you bitch!" Tameka said as she ran up on Lil J and started swinging.

Lil J backed up and gave her a hard back hand that sent her to the floor. "Dumb ass bitch. I'm outta here!"

"Naw wait. Don't leave me. Please don't leave me. I love you."

"Fuck you bitch!" Lil J said as he left.

When Lil J got out to his car he tried to call the number that was blowing him up and got the voice mail. When he tried a second time and got the same results, he checked his voice mail and saw that Beautyful had left him a message letting him know that she had the pizza and that he forfeited by not being on the block and not answering his phone. "Fuck" he hollered as he started his car and pulled off.

CHAPTER 13

The next day Lil J made it to the hood at ten in the morning. He was hoping to catch Beautyful before she left the crib, but unfortunately she was already gone so he chirped Zed and Reggie and told them to meet him at the pancake house out in Matteson, Illinois, so they could discuss their financial and security matters.

When they all met up at the pancake house Lil J and Zed ordered T-bone steaks, blueberry pancakes, scrambled eggs with cheese, hash browns and orange juice. While Reggie ordered turkey sausage links, waffles, scrambled eggs with cheese, toast and grape juice.

"Reggie, tell me how it's looking now that we started back fucking with dude." Lil J asked.

"It's looking real good." Reggie said before taking a sip of his grape juice. "If things keep moving like they moving then we gon' see about a extra 10 to 15 stacks on Vail and 5 to 10 on the 9."

"That's what's up. When was the last time you took care of our lawyers?" You know we gotta make sho' we keep them right."

"We ain't gotta worry about them. They about two fifty in the rear with us. Remember I been taking care of them since Slim put Zed up on them back in '99."

"Dude and them what's happening. They suppose to be hooking me up with a civil suit lawyer so I can file my law suit.

"How much you think you gon' get out that shit?" Reggie asked before he stuffed some eggs into his mouth.

"I don't know man, but them jailhouse lawyers back at the county was talking like a nigga could get some mills out that shit." Lil J said as he cut a piece from his steak and drowned it with A-1 sauce before banging it.

"Ay ya'll know that nigga Rick throwing a party at his club next week right?" Zed asked.

"Nah, I ain't heard about that." said Lil J.

"Yeah, he was suppose to be throwing a Fourth of July party, but he pushed it back a week because his bitch was tripping."

"Ya'll know what? I ain't never knew who his main bitch was."

"Nah?"

"Hell nah."

"Man that lame gotta bad ass bitch name Dollicia, and she fuck with bitches."

"Yeah?"

"Hell yeah." Zed said as Lil J's phone started going off.

"What up?" Lil J asked as he answered his phone.

"Hello, is this Lil J?" A female asked.

"Who wanna know?" Lil J asked wondering who the woman could be.

"Hold on." The woman said as she clicked over.

"Hello – Hello – Trina." Some nigga hollered through the phone.

"What?"

"Is he on the phone?"

"I don't know. Somebody on there tho', but I don't know if it's him."

"Ay cuz." The guy hollered.

"What up? Who is this?" Lil J asked.

"This Lunitic. Where Lil J at?"

"Aw what up Tic? This me nigga. What's happening?"

"Shit, I just came from court today and these bitches done fucked up and gave me a bond."

Lil J thought about the case that Lunitic had and knew that his bond had to be sky high. He was locked up for a murder on some niggas in his hood and two attempted murders on the police. He claimed that when the police came into his crib to lock him up for the body, he tried to shoot his way out.

After two officers got shot he ended up getting hit four times in the chest and twice in the arms. But fortunately for him he had on his bullet proof vest, because that was the only thing that saved his life.

"So where they put yo shit at?" Lil J asked.

"It's up there man. 250 to walk."

"Damn, how much you got?"

"I got 40, and a few of my guys say they gon' put together a 100 for me."

"Shit, you still need like 110."

"I know, but I'm gon' tryda get a few of my bitches to come up with something. I'm tryna be outta this bitch before December."

"You gon' come fuck with me when you get out in December?" Lil J asked. He knew that Lunitic wanted him to put up the one ten, and even though he was going to put it up, he wanted to fuck with him before he let him know that he had him.

Lunitic chuckled before he responded. "Yeah man, I'ma come fuck with you." He said sounding disappointed.

"Nah I'm just fucking with you. I'ma put up the one ten. Just give me my shit back when you get out."

"Come on bruh, you already know I got you."

"Aight, I got that paper right now, so whenever yo people ready just have them hit my phone.

"This my cousin Trina on the line. If my guys get that money together by the end of the night, she gon' call you in the morning."

"I'll be waiting on her call."

"Aight Lil J be cool out there. Love."

"Love." Lil J said as he got off the phone.

"What's up Lil J? What that shit was all about?" Reggie inquired.

Reggie and Zed were kicking bullshit back and forth until they heard Lil J say something about putting up the one ten.

"Do ya'll remember when I told ya'll that I had somebody take care of them niggas that stabbed me up?"

"Yeah." Reggie said while Zed nodded his head.

"That was him on the phone. He say he need me to help his peoples reach for him because the judge finally gave him a bond."

"How much is it?" Reggie inquired.

"Two hundred and fifty to walk."

"And you plan on dropping one ten on it?"

"Yeah, that's my man, but how my paper gon' look after that?"

"Aw you still gon' be decent. Remember you stacked some nice change while you was locked up.

"What type of case dude got?" Zed asked.

"A body and two attempts, but the attempts on the police."

"Damn, cuz be getting down like that?"

"Yeah, dude a beast." Lil J said as he told them the story about how Lunitic got locked up. After he finished, Reggie spoke up.

"So...who you gon' get to post the bond?"

"My white bitch."

"You talking about the one that fuck with the real estate?"

"Yeah, I'ma have her take care of that shit for me."

❧

Later on that night, Lil J and Zed were rolling through Harvey in a rental. The rental was a dark blue Maxima with tinted windows.

They were riding around hollering about all of the hitters and go getters in the hood. They knew that a lot of niggas were going to turn against them once the war that they knew was inevitable kicked off with Rick, so they wanted to plan ahead.

"Aight Zed, we already took care of these clowns over here, so we ain't even gotta worry about them. But out of all of the sets in the hood, who all do you think gon' side with Rick once the shit hits the fan?" Lil J asked as he drove down 146 in Loomis and saw RIP flags where Donta and Tray were gunned down at.

"The niggas from the Village gon' ride with him because that's his shit. And the niggas from 152 in Loomis and the 4th don't' like us, so you know they gon' ride with him."

"Who you think gone ride with us?"

"We fuck with them cats from the Dark side, so they gon' ride with us. And I know yo man and them from the dead end gon' fuck with us."

"What about them niggas from the Rezzo's?" Lil J asked as he turned off Loomis onto 147th street going west towards Vail.

"I really don't know man. I mean them dudes get down, but they X's guys, so you gon' have to ask him about them"

"Shit, if they X's guys, then nine times out of ten they gon' ride with us. But what's up with the other sets like page, union, Winchester, and the niggas from Dixmoor?"

"I don't know about the cats from them sets. They might be on some, I don't wanna get in ya'll war type of shit."

"And that's exactly the type of shit that I ain't gon' be try'na hear, because them niggas a be the ones that set us up when we least expect it. So it's either they with us or against us." Lil J said as he turned off 147th street onto Vail. When he pulled up to the apartment buildings, he saw Beautyful parking her car in the back parking lot. "Ay Zed, look at Beautyful ass back there in the parking lot."

"I see her, but fuck that. K. B told me that you was on some soft ass shit the other day when ya'll saw her at the gas station in Mid-low; say it ain't so?"

"That was Posen, but that's how that nigga got down on me?"

"Hell yeah,"

"It is what it is then." Lil J said as he parked the car and got out.

"Nah bruh it ain't." Zed said after he opened the passenger door and got out of the car.

"What you mean by that?" Lil J inquired as he turned around. His intentions were to go get up with Beautyful before she went in the house, but now he was curious to see what Zed was getting at.

"You wasting yo time try'na cuff shorty because in about another month and a half she gon' be gone to Georgia.

Lil J gave Zed a dubious look. "How you know that?"

"Her cousin Bianca told me."

"You talking about Bianca from Dixmoor?"

"Yeah, she told me that Beautyful got a scholarship from a college down there.

Aw yeah. Lil J thought as he fell deep in thought. At first he became discouraged when Zed told him that Beautyful was going to Georgia, but now that he knew the reason that she was going, he became avid. He was determined now more than he was before to get her and he wasn't about to let 400 plus miles stand in his way.

"Let's get out this street before the jumps roll up on us." Lil J said as him and Zed walked towards the buildings. When they made it through the gate they saw that Beautyful was standing on the balcony talking on her phone. "I'ma 'bout to go holler at shorty, I'ma get up with you in a minute."

"Aight man." Zed said as he watched Lil J go up the stairs.

"Baby girl, don't you know it's too dangerous for you to be out here on this balcony?"

Lil J asked as he interrupted Beautyful's phone call.

"Hold on girl." Beautyful said into the phone before she took it away from her ear. "Lil J, what I tell you about calling me Baby Girl? I ain't yo baby."

"Not yet."

Beautyful smiled. She was beginning to like Lil J, even though she didn't want to. She was leaving the State in a couple of months and didn't want to have a long distance relationship that she knew wouldn't last. "You confident ain't you."

"Very."

Beautyful smiled again. "Anyway, you rude. Can't you see I'm on the phone?"

"Tell them you a call back, I need to talk to you."

"And if I don't?"

"Then I'ma post up right here until you do." Lil J said as he leaned against the buildings and folded his arms.

This boy something else, she thought before she pulled the phone back up to her ear. "Bianca I'll call you back later." She said before ending the call. "Now what you want?"

"Where my pizza at?"

"I ate it."

"You ain't save me none?"

"Nope."

"So you just was gon' let me starve yesterday wasn't you."

"Naw boy. I called you three times and you didn't answer not once. So I figured you was cool. But thank you for fixing my car, filling my gas tank, buying me pizza, and stealing my car."

Lil J laughed. "That was the only way that it was gon' get fixed. But you ain't gotta thank me. That shit ain't nothing."

"It might not have been nothing to you, but it was a lot to me because I would've had to wait a whole two weeks before I would've had enough to fix it. And who told you where I worked?"

"The streets."

"Mmhm. You lucky the police ain't catch you stealing my car."

"I ain't worried about them. Besides, I ain't the one who stole it. I just paid for it to get fixed." Lil J said as an awkward silence fell upon them as he thought about what he wanted to say next. He didn't want to come on too strong because he didn't want her to look at him like the rest of the niggas in the hood. And plus he knew that her cousin probably gave her the 411 on him and let her know that he was a playa. But that must not have deterred her because if it would've he didn't think that she would be giving him as much play as she was giving him.

"What you go to jail for back in 2005?" Beautyful asked breaking the silence. She already knew the answer to the question, but she wanted to see if he was going to lie.

Damn she bold. "Who told you I went to jail back in '05?" he asked.

"The streets!" she said mimicking him.

"What else did the streets tell you about me?" Lil J asked trying to change the subject. He really didn't want to scare her off by telling her that he was locked up for killing three people. But little did he know, she already knew.

"Don't try'da change the subject nigga, answer my question."

"You a woman that likes to be in control ain't you?"

"As a matter of fact, I am." Beautyful said as she walked up closer to him. "Is that a problem?"

Damn she smell good. Lil J thought as he inhaled the perfume that was coming off Beautyful's body. "Nah Baby Girl. It ain't no problem. But what's this I'm hearing about you leaving me and going to Georgia?"

"What you mean leaving you? I barely even know you."

"See that's the problem I'm having right there."

"What you mean?"

"I wanna get to know you before you leave."

"What would be the point? I mean, I don't plan on coming back out here no time soon after I leave. And I'm not with that long distance relationship stuff. That's one of the main reasons why I don't have a boyfriend now."

"What are some of the other reasons?"

"I'ma tell you the reasons why I don't mess with street niggas. Ya'll too dangerous, and messing with ya'll is risky. And most of ya'll are players anyway. Straight Dogs."

"All street niggas ain't dogs Baby Girl."

Beautyful chuckled.

"Lil J you better stop while you're ahead because I done heard all about you."

"Anybody ever told you to believe nothing of what you hear, and half of what you see?"

"Nah, why?"

"Because believing what the streets say a make you miss out on a lot."

"Who said I believe?"

"So what you saying? You don't?"

"I don't know."

Lil J looked deep into Beautyful's eyes trying to find meaning, but instead found confusion. He could tell that she was feeling him, but something was holding her back.

"Stop looking at me like that." she said as she turned her back to him. The way that he was looking into her eyes was making her nervous. It felt as if he were looking into her soul.

"Why you so contained Baby Girl?" he asked.

Beautyful didn't respond. She was deep in thought trying to decide whether or not she should let Lil J into her life. She was really feeling him, but she didn't want to get hurt like her cousin and so many of their friends did in the past. They all had forewarned her about guys like Lil J, and let her know that they weren't any good. But right now, her heart was telling her different. So she felt like she was stuck between a rock and a hard place.

"Beautyful, all I wanna do is get to know you."

"Is that all you want to do?" Beautyful asked as she turned around.

"Not really."

"I thought so. But I'm getting tired of standing out here so I'ma 'bout to go in the house. I'ma consider what we talked about and think about calling you tomorrow."

"My conversation must've become insipid."

"What?"

"You tired of talking to me?"

"Nah silly. I'm just tired of standing out here."

"Aight, give me a hug before you go in then." Lil J said opening his arms. When Beautyful walked into his embrace he wrapped his arms around her and got another pleasing smell of her perfume. Dat gotta be Dolce and Gabbana.

After Lil J watched Beautyful go in the house, he went and kicked it with Zed and J. J for awhile before heading out to his baby mama's house.

When he pulled up to Karina's crib, all he was thinking about was going in the house and laying down next to her warm body, but just as he was about to go in the house, he got a call from Beautyful. "What's up Baby Girl" I thought you said you was gone call me tomorrow?" he asked as he pulled his .45 out of his back pocket and held it inside of his hoodie pocket before walking back over to his car.

"I still am, but I couldn't sleep so I decided to call you. Is that a problem?"

"Naw naw, that ain't a problem at all." Lil J said as he smiled and leaned on his car. Him and Beautyful conversed for two hours before his phone went dead.

CHAPTER 14

The next day Lil J woke up around 2 in the afternoon to an empty house. He didn't plan on sleeping in so late, but hell, he needed the rest.

Karina had to drop Malik off at her mother's house and be at work at 1:30 so she left the house at 12:00

After Lil J got out of bed and took care of his number one. He grabbed his phone and saw that he had eight missed calls, two of which were from Beautyful. She left a message letting him know that she really enjoyed their conversation last night and that she was looking forward to hearing from him after she got off work. The other six calls were from Trina, Lunitic's cousin. She left three voicemails telling him that she had the one forty and was ready to go get Lunitic whenever he was.

That nigga guys must've got right on top of business last night. Lil J thought as his phone started going off. When he looked at the screen he saw that it was Trina. "What's up?" he answered.

"Don't what's up me nigga!" Trina snapped. "I been calling yo ass since nine this morning. And my cousin been calling me since eight running up my damn phone bill!"

"My fault Trina baby. I was asleep, but you ain't gotta be tripping like that." Lil J said not liking how Trina was trying to check him.

"Is you ready to go get my cousin?"

"You got somebody legit enough to go get him?"

"Naw, my cousin told me that you was gonna take care of all of that. I mean you do got somebody right?" Trina asked sounding worried.

"Yeah I got it. But let me hop in the shower and get dressed. I should be ready around five. And if Lunitic call back tell him I said to be easy we got him."

"He ain't gonna call back. The county put a block on my phone because he called too much today already."

"Aight, I'ma hit you up later then." Lil J said as he ended the call before calling his vet broad Linzy, who was real deep up in the real estate game.

"Real Estate Linzy. How can I help you?" Linzy answered.

Lil J had called her on her business phone.

"I'm with Satisfaction Guaranteed Construction, and the only way that you can help me is if you let me come over there and tear down your walls."

Linzy was taken aback, so she took the phone away from her ear and looked at it before putting it back. "Excuse me?"

"You heard what I said C. Q. I ain't stutter."

"Aw hi baby!" Linzy said as her befuddlement turned into excitement. At first she was ready to go off until he called her C. Q. which meant Caucasian Queen. It was a nickname that Lil J had given her awhile back. "Why did you take so long to call me? You had me worried sick about you. I called the county jail last week and they told me that you were released a week prior."

"You was worried about me for real?"

"Yes I was. I was beginning to think that you left town or something."

"Nah, I just got a lot of shit that needs taken care of that's all. But you know I wouldn't leave town without my C. Q."

"You better not." she said as Lil J charmed her. "When am I gonna be able to see you?"

"Today."

"Oh, are you for real?"

"Yeah, I miss you. Plus I need you to take care of something for me."

"John, is this the only reason that you called me?" Linzy asked feeling like Lil J only wanted to use her.

"Nah, I called you because I wanted to spend some time with my C. Q. But I also need something taken care of. I mean I could get somebody else to take care of it for me, but I already told you that I need you to take care of it, now are you denying me?"

"Of course not."

"Good, and stop calling me John, its Lil J. But anyway I need you to go to the bank and get a cashier's check for two hundred and fifty thousand."

"Oh my God! You got to be kidding me. Are you serious?"

"Yeah I'm serious. And I need you to go get it before four o'clock."

"Two hundred and fifty thousand. Gosh, what are you trying to do?" Linzy asked. She was becoming nervous.

Linzy was a thirty seven year old real estate agent that owned her own real estate company. She was a beautiful white woman with a banging body that she kept in shape by going to the gym daily. She met Lil J back in 2000 when he was seventeen and she was thirty. She had already had nine years of real estate experience and Lil J wanted to learn about the business, at least that's what he led her to believe.

Her office was located inside of a mini mall plaza out in River Oaks. And one day when Lil J and his guys were coming out of a fitted cap store, her Mariah Carey figure caught his eye. She was putting up a sign in the window that read:

Interested in owning your own property?

Give us a call.

Now Lil J didn't know anything about real estate, and he could've cared less about some property, but if it meant that he would be bumping into fine women like the one that he was looking at, then he was all for it.

After he let his guys know what he was on, he slid up in real estate Linzy and inquired about the sign that she had posted up.

He was dressed in a black and white Girbaud fit, but carried hisself like a gentleman, so she saw him as an aspiring young man. While she talked he listened intently and asked good questions. And when she asked him what he was trying to do, he told her that he had inherited a large sum of money and was trying to learn a little bit about the business before he started to buy she became more than happy to inform him.

After about an hour of supplying him with information, a customer walked in and interrupted them. Lil J was already ready to go because he had his guys outside waiting, but he assured her that he would be back in the morning.

The next day Lil J made it to her office ten minutes after she opened up. This made her see that he was very intrigued, so she started the day off by telling him how she got into the business.

She enjoyed his company so much that she continued to babble and before she knew it she was telling him about herself, and where she grew up. When she realized where the conversation had gone she smiled and got back to business. Soon they were interrupted by a potential customer.

Lil J was ready to get back to the hood anyway, so before he left he gave her his number and told her to give him a ring.

Throughout the next two weeks, Linzy and Lil J conversed at least once a night and ended up going out to lunch a few times.

Linzy knew that she was out of character for not keeping things on a business note with this mysterious guy who called himself John Leebo, but there was something about him that made her want to get personal. Maybe it was his swag or the ingeniousness of him.

Whatever it was, Lil J was happy that he had it because before he knew it, he was out in Olympia Fields, Illinois long stroking Linzy in her five hundred thousand dollar house.

"Linzy baby, what I tell you about asking so many questions?" Lil J asked responding to her question.

"I'm sorry baby, but come on now; we're talking about two hundred and fifty thousand dollars. Some people don't' even make that in five years."

"So what you saying? You don't trust me with yo money?" Lil J asked becoming vexed.

"No, I'm not saying that. It's just that – "

"It's just what?" he asked cutting her off. He was beginning to think that she didn't trust him anymore. So he decided to test her.

"Linzy, I need the two hundred and fifty thousand. Now is you gon' give it to me or not?"

Linzy fell silent for a minute to consider what Lil J was asking. She had been messing around with him for six and a half years now. And in those six and a half years he had broke her heart and mended it. He had made her happier than money, or any man her age had made her and she loved him for that. So she chose to listen to her heart. "I hope you doing something good with the money John."

Lil J smiled. He knew that she loved him and would do anything for him, but she had him worried for a minute. "Thank you. Now leave somebody else in charge of the office and go get the check. I should be over yo house in about an hour."

"Okay. But baby, you really need to leave those streets alone and come move in with me. Those streets and that money is not worth your life."

"Linzy baby." Lil J said stopping her before she gave him a big lecture.

"Okay, okay. I love you John."

"I love you too baby." Lil J said, telling her exactly what she wanted to hear before ending the call. He really liked Linzy and had feelings for her, but he just couldn't see hisself settling down with a white woman.

✿

An hour and a half later, Lil J was pulling up to Linzy's mini mansion out in Olympia Fields. He had already stopped at one of his safe houses on the way there and picked up the one ten that he needed. So now all there was left to do was to make sure that Linzy had the check and call Trina.

When Lil J exited his car and approached Linzy's front door, she flung it open, before he got a chance to knock, and jumped into his arms.

"Oh baby, I missed you so much!" she managed to get out in between the kisses that she was planting all over Lil J's face.

"Damn baby! You ain't even let me get a good look at yo sexy self. Back up some." Lil J said as he inhaled the pleasing aroma coming off Linzy's body.

"OOH I'm sorry." she said as she smiled and stepped back to let Lil J see what she was working with. She had her jet black hair pressed and laid down just the way he liked it, with her best all black Versace dress on that was complimented by her all black Versace heels that showed off her pretty toes. But what topped everything off was the Paris Hilton perfume that she knew he would love.

"My baby know just what to do to get me going don't you?" Lil J asked as he walked over and took Linzy back into his arms.

"Mmmhm." she said as she started kissing on him once again before he scooped her up and carried her into the house.

Lil J thought about his one ten that he left in the car, but disregarded it once he remembered where he was.

After he closed the door behind them, he carried Linzy up to her bedroom where they copulated for awhile before jumping into the shower.

When they got out of the shower and got dressed, Lil J sent Linzy out to his car to grab the one ten. He let her know that they would pick up the rest later.

While she was outside, he called Trina and told her to meet him at the county with the one forty in an hour before he called Zed and let him know what the business was. He trusted Lunitic and didn't think that he would pull anything slick, but there was no telling what his guys were going to be on after Trina gave him the one forty.

When Lil J and Linzy pulled up to the county jail in Linzy's Jolly Rancher Red Ferrari, they parked behind the black '06 Impala that Trina said she would be in. After Lil J hopped out of the passenger side of the Ferrari and walked over to the Impala, he saw that Trina brought two guys with her. He didn't become alarmed though because he knew that the two guys were probably just there to make sure that she didn't get robbed.

"You Trina right? Lil J inquired.

"Yeah, and you must be Lil J." Trina asked as she admired his looks.

"Yeah."

"You got the money?"

"Is that a rhetorical question?"

"Don't get smart." Trina said as she got out of her car.

Damn she got a fat ass. "Come on now Trina. A redundant question deserves a redundant answer."

"You talking to me as if you already know me or something."

Lil J shook his head. "It's already six thirty, so give me the one forty so we can go in here and post the bond."

Trina looked at him like he was crazy. "I ain't giving you nothing. We can go in there and post the bond together."

Lil J laughed. "Trina you think we about to walk in there with $250,000 cash and post his bond? You gotta be crazy. They a lock our ass up. My girl legit, she got a cashiers check that she gone bond him out with."

"Well I'll give you the money after she post the bond then. How's that?" Trina asked with a matter-o-fact look on her face.

Lil J looked up the block just in time to see X's truck turn the corner, and Zed was already parked a few cars behind Linzy's Ferrari. He had already told them to be ready to get it cracking if anything went wrong, so he said fuck it and decided to do thing's Trina's way. "Aight, but look, I ain't going in there. You can go in with my girl. But as soon as ya'll post the bond I want my one forty."

"Okay, I can see it that way."

"Linzy baby, come here." Lil J said as he watched Linzy get out of the car and approach him. "Baby this Trina. Trina this Linzy."

"Nice to meet you." Linzy said to Trina.

This fine ass nigga a sellout. Fuck he doing with this white bitch. "Hey." Trina said in a yeah whatever tone of voice.

Lil J sensed Trina's jealousy and smiled. "Linzy, she gon' go in there with you while you post my man bond. I'ma wait out here in the car."

"Okay baby." Linzy said as her and Trina walked across the street to Division 5.

Two hours later they were walking back out of Division 5.

"What happened?" Lil J asked as he got out of the Ferrari.

"Nothing, they said that he should be coming out in about an hour or two." Linzy said.

Trina went to her car and grabbed the one forty before she walked over and gave it to

Lil J. "Thank you Lil J. I really appreciate you helping my cousin."

"Don't worry about it." Lil J said before he gave Zed a signal. "Lunitic my man. When I needed him he came through for me, so I'm just returning the favor." he said before he handed Zep, who was on the passenger side of Zed's Infiniti, the black bag that contained the one forty.

"Aight bruh, see you in the hood." Zep said before they pulled off.

When Lunitic came out of Division 5 around 11:30, Lil J got out of the Ferrari and leaned against it while Trina went and greeted him. Two minutes later they were walking in his direction.

"What's up jo? What's good?" Lunitic hollered as him and Lil J embraced.

"You what's good nigga. What's happening?"

"Man a nigga glad to be up outta that bitch. That's what's happen'n."

"Right. That is what's happening. I know I was glad to get the fuck up out of there. But check this out." Lil J said as he pulled a stack of hundred dollar bills out of his pocket.

"Here go five racks for you to go shopp'n with."

"That's love baby, but what you been on?"

"Shit. It's a lot of bullshit going on in my hood right now. So I ain't really been on shit."

"Yeah?" Lunitic said as he looked over into the Ferrari at Linzy. "You good tho'?"

"Yeah, I'm good. And she off limits."

Lunitic smiled. "That's you?"

Lil J nodded his head. "That's my white vet broad I told you about."

"That's the same one that was in them pictures you showed me?"

"Yeah, but dig this, me and my guys is suppose to be hitting this club next Saturday. This nigga we know throwing a party up there, you wanna roll?"

"What's today? Thursday. You ain't talking about the Saturday that's coming up is you?"

"Nah, the one after that."

"Aw hell yeah I wanna roll. But you know how I get down."

"Yeah I know." Lil J said as he smiled. "I feel the same way. I rather be with it then without it."

"I see it no other way."

"Come slide on me after you and yo people catch up on lost time. I got something for you." Lil J said as him and Lunitic embraced again before he hopped back in the car with Linzy.

"You ready?" Linzy asked.

"Yeah, take me out to my hood so I can pick up the rest of yo money."

"Is you staying with me tonight?" she asked as she put the car in drive and pulled off.

"I ain't gone be able to. I gotta take care of something." Lil J said thinking about Beautyful. She had called him while he was waiting on Lunitic, but he told her that he was busy and let her know that he would call her back. Now he couldn't get her off his mind.

"You still don't work on the weekends tho', right?"

"Nope."

"Aight, I'll be to see you tomorrow night then."

~

It had been two days since Wayne told Rick that Tank had called saying that him and his guys were getting impatient. And Rick knew that it was only a matter of time before they got fed up and did them, and he didn't need that, so he hopped into his Escalade along with Wayne, Calvin and one of his bodyguards and headed out to Robbins.

When they pulled into the old projects, Rick chirped Tank and let him know that he was around so that Tank could alert his guys. The last thing he wanted to do was catch a bullet that wasn't meant for him.

Calvin was driving the Escalade, so Rick told him to pull all the way to the middle of the projects where Tank usually parked his Navigator.

"Face, let that nigga in." Rick said as he watched Tank emerge from the cut.

When Face hopped out of the truck, Tank hopped in and closed the door.

"What it is Tank?" How life been treating you out here in the jects?" Rick inquired.

"Man fuck how life been treating me, let's talk about how you been treating me."

"Easy killa." Rick said as he smiled. "I know I been holding you back for awhile, but you gotta be patient."

"Man I been patient long enough. I feel like it's time to get it in there."

"Yo guys feel the same way?"

"Hell yeah, and I'm tired of holding my killas back."

"Aight, just be easy and give me about another week and a half."

"Aight man, but I'm telling you right now, another week and a half is all I'm giving you before me and my guys go do our thang."

"I respect that. But what's going on out here on the money side?" Rick asked, changing the subject.

"Come on now, this the projects. You know the money always looking good." Tank said, not really caring for the small talk. He had heard what he was trying to hear and was ready to dip back into the cut with his goons. "But I'll be to holler at you in a couple of days to get right." he said before he opened the door and stepped out of the truck.

"Aight, I'll be waiting on you." Rick said before his bodyguard got back into the truck and closed the door.

CHAPTER 15

When Next Saturday came around Lil J, Lunitic and the rest of Lil J's crew were up in Rick's club chilling and drinking on some Rosé until the bartender came over to their table with two bottles of Louie the XIII and an invitation to the VIP section. They accepted the L13, but declined the invitation.

They knew that they were showing blatant disrespect by declining the invitation, but they didn't give a fuck because they were strapped. X had paid the man at the door a couple of racks to let them in without being searched.

"That was love the way you put a nigga on his feet the other day." Lunitic said, referring to the brick of cocaine that Lil J hit him with a few days ago.

"That's wasn't shit bruh, I was just showing you my appreciation for what you did to them niggas for me when you got that kite I sent you."

Suspect was bemused for a minute before he remembered what Lil J was talking about. "You talking about them bitch ass niggas that hit you up at court?"

"Yeah."

"I did them niggas in something decent, didn't I?"

"Hell yeah you did. That shit made the news."

"I was scared as hell. I thought them niggas was gone tell them people on me."

"I'm – "

"Yo check out this lame over in VIP." Zed said cutting Lil J off.

When they all looked over to the VIP section, they saw Rick and his guys chilling with a flock of bad bitches.

"That must be dude and them that sent them drinks over." said Lunitic.

"It is, but the nigga in the white suite is the head of them clowns." K. B said before taking a sip of his drink.

"What's up with that nigga?"

"A lot." said Lil J. "That bitch ass nigga tried to have me changed the day I came home. But the niggas that he paid to do it came up missing before they got a chance to get at me, if you know what I mean."

Lunitic knew exactly what Lil J meant. And he was becoming madder and madder as

Lil J was filling him in on the type of shit that Rick was on. "So what's up with this dude? Why the fuck is he still breathing?"

"Because it ain't that simple. The nigga a king on these streets and he well connected. Don't you know that flavor that I gave you the other night?" Lil J asked, referring to the cocaine.

"Yeah, what about it?"

"Guess where it came from."

"Hold up! So you telling me that this nigga tried to have you whacked, and instead of getting down on him, you start fucking with him? That shit don't make no sense to me man. Ya'll niggas out here in Harvey backwards." Lunitic said before he leaned back in his chair and took a swig of the L13 that was in his cup.

"It'll make sense to you if I broke it down, but it's too much of a long story, so I'm just gone say that it is a means to an end, and leave it at that. But watch that Harvey shit. You and them niggas from the chi did enough of that shit while I was in the county."

Lunitic fell out laughing.

Over in the VIP section, Rick, Wayne, and Calvin were chilling hard, but not as hard as they were chilling before Lil J and his guys showed up. But Rick didn't want Lil J to get the wrong impression, so he sent two bottles of L13 along with an invitation to the VIP section over to their table, hoping that it would show Lil J that he was past all of the bullshit.

But when he got word that Lil J turned down his invitation, he wanted to send a few of his goons over to get down on him. But he had to be smart, plus he didn't want anything to go down inside of his club. So he told Wayne to call Tank and tell him to come be on point for when Lil J and his guys left the club.

Twenty minutes later, Wayne's phone started vibrating. "Ay Rick, this Tank right here." Wayne said after he looked at his caller I.D. "See where he at and if he outside go out there and let him know what's up.

"What up?" Wayne asked as he answered his phone.

"I'm on the scene man. What the business is?"

"I'ma 'bout to come out and holler at you."

"Aight." Tank hung up.

Zed had been watching the VIP section ever since he spotted Rick and his guys. He knew that something was bound to go down from the way that they turned down Rick's invitation, so he wanted to be on point. He knew that Rick was about to get on some bullshit because he had just watched him and Wayne exchange words before Wayne hopped on his cell phone, but what confirmed everything was when Wayne got up and left out of the club.

"I think these niggas is about to try'da pull a stunt." said Zed.

"Shit, I wouldn't put it past them because if a nigga turned down my invitation, I'd be ready to pull a stunt too. But it ain't shit, all we gotta do is be on point from here on out and we should be good." Lunitic said as he looked around.

Lil J picked up his cup and drank the rest of the L13 that was inside of it before he stood up. "Fuck them niggas they ain't on shit. And if they is we ain't about to sit here and let them catch us slipping. So if they really want us, they know where to find us. Lets ride." He said as him and his guys headed towards the door. When they got out to the parking lot and hopped in their whips, they never peeped Tank and Wayne hollering inside of a Lumina with tinted windows.

When Tank saw Lil J and his guys leaving the club, he hit Tone on the chirp. "Ay cuz, them niggas coming ya'll way so be looking out."

"What they riding in?" came back through the chirp.

"A Beemer, a Lac truck, and a Charger."

"Aight."

"Tank, make sho' you get that nigga man. And be careful." Wayne said as he opened the door and got out of the car.

"Aight I got you." Tank said before Wayne closed the door.

When Tank pulled out of the parking lot, he made a right onto 147th street. "Cuz, ya'll see them niggas yet?" he asked as he hollered through his chirp again.

"Yeah, we on them right now."

"Aight, I'm on my way." Tank said as he continued riding west on 147th street.

Three minutes later Tone chirped his phone.

"Ay T, it look like these niggas about to go through they hood, and I think it'll be kinda crazy to try'da get down on them over there knowing that they got all of them shorties posted up out there with them choppers."

"I feel you, but just keep following them and if they go through there, just fall back in the cut and wait on me."

"Aight."

❦

Back at the club, Greg was pulling up just as Wayne was sending Snake, one of his soldiers from the village, behind Tank. He told Snake to stay his distance and to keep his eyes open and to report back to him asap if something went down.

"What up with the urgent call Wayne?" Greg asked as him and P'nut emerged from P'nut's 750 Li BMW.

"Man you about five minutes too late."

"Yeah?"

"Hell yeah. That nigga who we talked about the other day was just up here, and I wanted to show you who he was."

"What the fuck was he doing up here?"

"Kicking it nigga, what else, but check this out. If you still try'na scope him out, it's a bitch inside the club that he used to fuck with hard. Maybe you or ya man can get something out the hoe."

"How she look?"

"She right."

"This mu'fucka packed. What ya'll got going on up here?" P'nut inquired after looking around the parking lot.

"My man threw a party."

"Aw ya'll don't fuck with us Chicago Heights niggas huh?"

"Knock that shit off and come on in here man." Wayne said before he turned around and walked into the club. After he took Greg and P'nut to the VIP section to briefly greet Rick, he made his way over to the dance floor and showed them Tameka and Aliana.

"That's dude old bitch right there in the red dress." he said nodding his head towards Tameka. She was dancing all up on Aliana while a small crowd stood watching.

"That bitch got a fat ol' ass." said Greg. "Dude don't fuck with her no more?"

"He might be fucking her here and there, but I don't think he fuck with her like he use to."

"What's her name?"

"Tameka."

"Who is that bitch she dancing with?" P'nut inquired.

"That's her friend Aliana."

"Dem hoes bi?"

"Not to my knowledge. I think they just doing that for the attention." Wayne said as he watched Tameka and Aliana stumble off the dance floor and make their way over to the bar.

"Me and my man about to go see what we can get out of these hoes." Greg said hoping that he would be able to come up on some pussy and information. "Drinks on the house right?"

"Everything but the L13."

"Aight we a get up with you later." Greg said before him and P'nut headed to the bar.

"That was a nice performance that ya'll put on out there on the dance floor." he said as he walked up and stood behind Tameka. "Put whatever these ladies drinking on me." he told the bartender.

Tameka looked back at Greg and smiled before turning back towards the bartender. *All this nigga try'na pay to play huh.* Well let's see how much he willing to spend. "If he paying for whatever we drinking, then you can scratch that Hennessy and bring us some Louie the XIII." she said before she turned and winked at Aliana.

Thirsty ass expensive bitch. Greg thought as he cracked a smile. *Dis bitch better be glad that I need something from her.*

༄

Riding down 147th street, Lunitic was driving Lil J's BMW while Lil J was on the passenger side listening to Jeezy's Cain't Band the Snow Man with his .45s on his lap. Reggie, Mikey, and X were right behind them in X's truck. While Zed, Zep, and K. B were picking up the rear in Zep's Charger.

When Lunitic put on his left turn signal and was about to go through Lil J's hood, Mikey alerted his phone.

"Yo." Lunitic hollered through his chirp after turning the radio down.

"Ay pull in the liquor store up there real quick."

"Aight." Lunitic said as he turned off his turn signal and pulled into the right lane. Before K. B. was able to pull into the lane behind him, a dark blue conversion van pulled up and closed the space.

Had they not been off their square from the Rosé and L13, they probably would have noticed that the van and two other cars took turns following them all the way from the club.

When Lunitic pulled into the liquor store parking lot, the van pulled in right behind him and that's when Zed saw that something was up, but it was too late because before he could say or do anything, Tone and three of his guys were already hopping out of the van unloading clips inside of the BMW.

Lunitic managed to slide out of the car with his D-eagle without being hit, but Lil J on the other hand wasn't so fortunate. Because as he tried to dive out of the door behind Lunitic, he caught a slug to the back of his shoulder.

When Lunitic hopped up to throw a few slugs back at his assailants, he raised up just in time to see Zed chop two of 'em down with an AR-15.

"Yeeeeah!" Lunitic hollered as he let his D-eagle ride, catching another one of their assailants in the chest, fatally wounding him.

When Tone saw that things weren't going his way, he tried to jump back into the van but was cut down by the Mac 11's that Mikey and Reggie ran up spraying.

"Yo Lil J, you aight over there?" Mikey asked thinking that they had everything under control.

"Watch out!" Lil J hollered as he lifted the .45 in his left hand and let it holler.

When Mikey turned around to see what Lil J was shooting at, his whole world turned black as a bullet slammed into the side of his forehead.

Mack had pulled into the parking lot just in time to see Tone get hit up, and as he saw his body hit the ground he hopped out of the car that he was in with a SKS and ran amok.

Reggie had caught a few slugs from the SKS too, but was laying on the ground still breathing. X and K. B were close by him and Mikey when they got hit up and knew that Mikey was gone from the size of the chunk missing from his head. They also knew that Reggie was going to be gone too if they didn't hurry up and get him out of the line of fire.

"X get Reggie!" K. B hollered as he came from behind the Charger letting two 40s ride at Mack and the rest of the niggas that jumped out of his whip.

"Ahhhfuck!" Mack hollered as he dropped the SKS and dipped behind his car. When he looked at his right hand he saw blood coming out of a nub where his middle finger used to be. "OL' bitch as nigga!" he hollered as he pulled a .357 out of his pocket.

Just as X pulled Reggie out of the line of fire, Tank and Rob pulled into the parking lot on bullshit.

"K. B get back!" Lunitic hollered as he started firing the .45 that Lil J handed him after he emptied his D-eagle.

While K. B was running trying to get out of the line of fire he was hit in the back by a few buck shots from the Mossberg that Tank ran up blasting.

"X, put Reggie in the truck so we can get the fuck out of here!" Zep hollered as he dropped the empty AK and started firing the two 9's that he pulled from his waist band. Zed had run over with his AR-15 and helped Zep cover X while he put Reggie in the truck.

"Lil J, bring yo bitch ass from behind that car nigga!" Tank hollered as he continued to rock the night with his Mossberg.

"Lets ride before them people get here." Mack hollered.

"Yeah, let's ride before we go to jail fucking with these niggas." Rob said still firing his Mack 10.

When Tank heard the sirens in the distance indicating that the police were coming, he started crawfishing. "Aight, let's get the fuck outta here then." he said before he went and hopped back into his whip.

When Lil J saw Tank and his guys leaving, he hollered over to X and told him to take Reggie to the hospital.

"We need to get you to a hospital too." Lunitic said to Lil J as he helped him into the car.

"Hell nah, I ain't going to no hospital so they can lock me up. Just take me out to my

B. M crib."

As Lunitic was about to hop in the car, he looked over and saw Zed and Zep checking out K. B's back. "What's up Zed? He cool?"

"Nah, he got hit in the back a few times."

"Come ride with us K. B. Zed, you and Zep go lay low. I'ma be out in Thorton if ya'll need me." said Lil J.

"What about Mikey?" Zep asked.

When Lil J looked down at Mikey's lifeless body tears came to his eyes and he felt a sense of resentment. "He already gone Zep. It ain't nothing we can do for him."

"Lil J, we gone slide through yo block and hop in my whip. This mu' fucka too messed up to be rolling in." Lunitic said as he pulled off after K.B got in the car.

CHAPTER 16

    The liquor store that Lil J and his guys were trying to go to was located inside of a small town next to Harvey called Dixmoor. The population in the town was only about 3 to 4 thousand so the police force was small with only a few officers on duty at a time. And half the time the officers that were on duty after midnight were either at a club chilling, or somewhere creeping with a bitch, like officer Jackson who was on duty was doing when his Sergeant radioed and told him to go see about a "shots fired" call at the liquor store.
    He was so avid to get his nut off from the head that he was receiving, that when the call came through he gave his Sergeant the 10-4 letting him know that he would check it out, then disregarded it as probably a call about late fireworks.
    Three minutes later his Sergeant radioed him again and told him to go to the liquor store immediately; so he concluded what he was doing with the underage hood rat and headed to the liquor store. When he finally made it up there and got out of his car to check out the situation, he was devastated by what he saw. It was a massacre. Dead bodies were lying in the parking lot, and cars were shot-up. He stood there looking at the bodies bemused for a minute before he radioed the situation in.
    Detectives Jones and Bradly pulled into the liquor store parking lot shortly after the ambulance got there. Officer Jackson had called and told them to come check out the situation because he knew that nine times out of ten the situation derived from something that happened in their district.
    "What's going on with you Jack? What the hell happened up here?" Detective Jones asked as him and Officer Jackson shook hands.

"I don't know, but whatever happened it wasn't good."

"Is anybody still breathing?" Detective Bradly asked after looking around at the dead bodies.

"Nope, we got five bodies and all of them D.O.A."

"Damn. You don't' mind if I go take a look around do you?"

"Nah, go ahead, but you know the rules, don't touch anything."

"Yeah, yeah. I know the rules." Detective Bradly said before he walked off.

"Did anybody up here see what happened? Detective Jones asked.

"Yeah, those two crack heads over there say they saw what happened, but the shit they told me doesn't make any sense."

While Officer Jackson was giving Detective Jones the run down on what the crack heads told him, Detective Bradly was viewing the dead bodies.

"Ay Jones, come and look at who I found." Detective Bradly said as he came across what was left of Mikey.

Damn! That explains a lot." Detective Jones said as he walked over and saw the hole in Mikey's head.

"Ya'll know this guy?" Officer Jackson asked.

"Yeah we know him. That's Michael Brown. Him and his guys hang out around the corner not too far from here." Detective Jones said as his phone started going off. "Hold on for a second while I take this call.

"Bradly, you know any of those other dead guys?" Officer Jackson asked.

"Nope, just this one. I ain't never seen any of them other guys, but – "

"Bradly, we gotta go to the hospital. Some guy was just brought in with multiple gunshot wounds to the body."

"Aight Jack, we gon' do some investigation and get back with you later." Detective Bradly said as him and Detective Jones got in their car and pulled off.

When they got to the hospital and found out that the guy that they were coming to see about was Reginald Gray, they knew that they were on to something, because Reginald Gray AKA Reggie was connected with Michael Brown AKA Mikey.

They also knew that whatever happened to Reggie had to happen at the liquor store. So they were hoping that he made it through surgery so that they could question him and find out what happened and see who else was involved.

When Lunitic made it out to Thorton on his way to drop Lil J and K. B off, Lil J called Karina and let her know that he was around the corner, and that him and his man were going to need some medical attention.

She tried to advise him to go to the hospital when he let her know that the medical attention was going to be needed for gunshot wounds, but he told her that he wasn't going to no hospital before ending the call.

When they got to the house and Karina saw all the blood on Lil J, she almost fainted. It wasn't seeing all of the blood that almost made her faint because by being a nurse she was used to seeing a lot of blood. But it was the person who the blood was coming from that made her almost lose her mind.

She love Lil J and never thought something so dramatic could happen to him, and she just couldn't bear the thought of losing him, so as those thoughts continued to flood her mind, she snapped back to the matter at hand and got to work.

When she cleaned all of the blood off him, she was relieved to see that it was only a flesh wound. After she was finished taking care of him, she checked out K.B and saw that he was cool other than the few buckshot pellets that were in his back. When she finished plucking the pellets from underneath his skin and cleaning him up, she walked out of the room.

Lil J and K.B stayed silent for awhile feeling nothing but grief. Rick and the niggas from Robbins had got it in there tonight. They had killed Mikey and shot up Lil J, K.B and Reggie. Yeah, they had scored big time. But Lil J knew that it was only a matter of time before they paid dearly for what they did to him and his people.

"K. B, call X and see what's up with Reggie." Lil J said as he broke the silence. "Then hit Zed up and let him and Zep know that we cool. Tell them I said to stay low until further notice."

"Aight." K. B said before he grabbed his phone off the night stand.

"What's up Lil J? What you on?" Lunitic asked as he walked into the room and closed the door behind him. He was out on the front porch making phone calls until Karina came and told him that she was done taking care of Lil J and K. B.

"What you mean…what I'm on? These niggas just got down on me and my guys, and changed one of my niggas. I'ma 'bout to kill these bitches, that's what I'm on!"

"Who the hell was dude that was hollering out yo name?"

"That bitch ass nigga name Tank. He from the old projects in Robbins where I caught my case at. Them niggas I changed out there was his guys."

"So this shit ain't got nothing to do with that lame at the club?"

"Hell yeah this got something to do with dude. How else you think them niggas got the scoop on us. That's probably what that nigga Wayne was out there doing when he left the club."

"Check this out, if you on what you say you on, then I got niggas that's ready to go out there tonight and get shit cracking."

"Nah, we ain't gone go out there tonight because it'll be a waste of time. You know them niggas probably somewhere lay'n low. So we just gon' fall back for awhile or at least until me and K.B heal up, because I wanna be close to 100% when we go out there so I can really do my thang."

"I'ma 'bout –"

"John, I need to see you in the other room for a minute." Karina hollered from the other side of the door.

"Aight, here I come." Lil J hollered back.

"What you was saying Tic?"

"I'ma 'bout to head out to the town. But make sho' you hit my phone and let me know what's up before you go out there and get down on them niggas."

"Aight, I got you bruh, but be careful out there."

"Look who talking." Lunitic said before he left.

"Ay Lil J, X said Reggie in surgery right now, and the doctors talking about they don't know if he gon' make it. He say he had to leave the hospital tho' because the nurses started asking too many questions and he didn't want to be there when the police showed up. He said he called Mikey's sister and let her know the deal too."

"Did he let her know that we gone finance the funeral?"

"Yeah, he say he told her that we gon' pay for everything, but she wasn't trying to hear that shit."

Lil J nodded his head.

"What was Zed talking about?"

"Shit, I told him what you said tho'."

"I'ma 'bout to go see what shorty want."

"Aight, I got this bitch Rella from 95th coming to pick me up. I'ma chill with her for awhile."

"I'ma hit yo phone if I need you." Lil J said before he walked out of the room.

When Lil J entered Karina's bedroom and saw her lying in the bed, he thought that she was asleep until he heard the sniffles that let him know that she was crying.

"Karina baby, what's wrong?" he asked as he caressed her shoulder with his left hand.

"John." Karina started as she managed to stop crying for a second. "I love you, but I – ." Was all that she could get out before she started crying again. But just hearing those few words were enough to let Lil J know what was wrong.

Karina was in love with him and she feared what every other female that messed with street niggas feared. So as she sat there crying uncontrollably, Lil J did the best he could at consoling her.

CHAPTER 17

Out in Robbins, Tank and his guys were mad and going crazy over losing Tone and three of their troops. They were trying to figure out why Tone had taken it upon himself to move without them. Tank was madder about losing Tone than anything else because Tone was his cousin, and his aunt had made him promise her that he would always watch over and protect Tone. But now that Tone was dead, he didn't know how he was going to deliver the bad news to her.

"Fuck!" Tank hollered as he punched a hole into the wall.

"Ay, ya'll don't think that them niggas peeped us following them and then got down on Tone when they saw that we wasn't around?" Rob asked as he fired up a swisher.

"Hell nah I don't think them niggas peeped us, because if that was the case, they probably woulda just went through they hood where they got niggas on standby instead of going to the liquor store risking what just happened. Plus I don't think them two niggas that I chopped down woulda let me catch them slipping like I caught them if they woulda peeped us." Mack responded before he took a long swig of the Hennessy that he was drinking straight to ease the pain in his finger that the car cigarette lighter left.

"So Tone must've just jumped out of the van and tried to get down on dude and them thinking that shit was sweet huh?" Red asked as he grabbed the blunt from Rob. Him, B.C Steve, and Lil Bill had stayed in the hood holding the projects down while Tank and the rest of the guys went out to Harvey.

"That nigga had to man, because as soon as I was pulling up I saw them niggas getting down on him."

"Damn!" Why the fuck this nigga couldn't just wait on us man!" Tank snapped more to himself than anybody else.

"We gotta get rid of dude because we losing too many guys fucking with him." Said A. P.

"Nigga what the fuck you think we been trying to do?" Rob snapped. "You think we playing with these niggas or something?"

"Naw, I'm just saying -."

"Well quit just saying nigga! Fuck you mean!"

"Fuck I mean. Nigga - ."

"Both of you niggas need to calm the fuck down because right now ain't the time for that bullshit. We got more important shit that we need to be focused on like getting the troops together and going to finish dude and the rest of his niggas off." Tank said as someone alerted his phone. "What up?" he hollered through his chirp.

"Wayne out here in an Escalade."

"Aight tell him I'll be out there in a minute." Tank said before he took the phone away from his mouth. "Ay ya'll come outside and get on security while I go holler at this lame." he said as him and his guys headed out to the parking lot.

"What's up? What you need to holler at me about?" Tank asked after hopping in Wayne's truck.

"What the fuck happened out there?" Wayne asked. He already knew what happened though because as soon as Tank left the club, he sent Snake, one of his soldiers from the village, right behind him. He told Snake to stay his distance and keep his eyes open and to report back to him asap if something went down. So as soon as the drama at the liquor store was over with, Snake came back to the club and let him, Calvin and Rick know what unfolded. Rick became furious at first when he heard Snake say that Lil J was still breathing, but calmed hisself down once he realized the danger that he was in. He had sent Tank and his guys to get down on Lil J and they missed, and he knew that it was only a matter of time before Lil J found out that he was involved. So he needed time to clear his mind so that he could think straight, but in the meantime he sent Wayne out to the projects to see what Tank's story was.

"I don't know man. Shit just got fucked up." Tank said as he responded to Wayne's question.

"What you mean?"

"I lost four guys tonight and one of them was my cousin Tone. He jumped out of his car try'na get Lil J while me and the rest of my guys wasn't around." Tank said while shaking his head. "My man Mack say he pulled up just in time to see my Lil cousin get cut in half by the choppers that two of Lil J's guys was shooting."

"Did ya'll get any of them niggas?" Wayne asked not really caring about Tank's losses.

"Yeah, we chopped two of them cats down."

"Aight that's cool. I mean it's a start. But anyway, what you plan on doing now?"

"I'ma 'bout to get all of my goons together and go out here and find that nigga. I lost too many guys to dude. It's time for this shit to end. And you can tell Rick that I ain't honoring no more red lights, it's all green from here on out. It ain't nothing he can do or say to stop me." Tank said before he opened the door and stepped out of the truck.

"Yo Tank."

"What up?" Tank asked as he stopped and looked back.

"I understand man, and if that's how you feel, then it is what it is."

Tank didn't respond, he just nodded his head before closing the door.

"Rick." Wayne hollered through his phone as he chirped Rick.

"Speak."

"I just got through talking to ya boy."

"And?"

"I think we need reinforcements."

"You know what to do then."

"Is my boy still there?"

"Nah, he left with shorty."

"Aight." Wayne hollered back through his chirp before he called Greg.

༺༻

After Greg and P'nut talked Tameka and Aliana into leaving the club, they headed over to Tameka's crib where she decided to let the freak out. She was drunk and feeling herself, so her and Greg dipped off into her bedroom and left Aliana and P'nut in the living room.

As soon as Greg got into the bedroom, he stashed his .357 under one of the pillows on the bed and laid back on it and watched Tameka do a little drunk strip tease. When she took off her red D & G mini dress he admired her curvaceous body.

Her perky breasts looked edible as she unsnapped her bra and let them fall freely. When she pulled off her white thong and made her ass clap, Greg's dick became so hard that he damn near burst through his pants.

I'ma 'bout to fuck the shit outta this bitch, Greg thought as he started to undress.

Tameka's pussy was soaking wet and she was ready to get her freak on, so she walked over and climbed into the bed before she took Greg's dick into her mouth and started bobbing while playing with his balls at the same time.

What the fuck! Greg thought as Tameka stopped sucking his dick and tried to get up and straddle him. "Hold up Lil mama." he said as he stopped her and put a condom on. "Aight come on Ma. Let's get it."

Tameka gave Greg a dubious look before she straddled him and began riding like a pro. She didn't like having sex with condoms because they took the feeling out of it, but she didn't really know Greg so she made an exception.

Tameka's pussy was feeling so good to Greg that he felt hisself about to cum, but before he did, Tameka came and his phone started ringing at the same time.

"Get up ma." he said.

When Tameka rolled off him and laid on her back, he got up and grabbed his phone out of his pants. "What up?" he answered already knowing that it was Wayne from the ringtone.

"I need you to take care of that issue."

"You know I'ma need a hundred right?"

"Fifty now and fifty later."

"I'll be to get it in the morning." Greg said before he ended the call. He hadn't got any information out of Tameka about Lil J yet, but he knew that he would in due time. "Come on ma." He said as he grabbed Tameka's hand and pulled her out of the bed before bending her over and entering her from behind. He peeped the tattoo that read "This belongs to" on her lower back and "Lil J" on her ass cheeks and made a mental note of it before he began dog fucking her, causing her to moan in bliss. When he smacked her on her fat ass she moaned louder and started throwing it back at him.

Greg became impressed by how well Tameka's thick ass was taking the dick and started pounding her out until he exploded.

CHAPTER 18

Over the next few days, Lil J stayed out at his baby mama's house trying to let his shoulder heal up while his guys were laying low in the hood.

Zed had put J. J, Ant and the rest of the shorties in the hood up on what went down at the liquor store and told them to be on point just in case the niggas from Robbins started coming through on bullshit.

He also let them know to call him if something went down, but so far nothing had happened. J. J still called him though, to let him know that everything was good, and to tell him that the niggas from Robbins had been coming through but weren't on anything.

Reggie had made it through surgery and was in the intensive care unit. The doctors said that one of the bullets damaged his spinal cord so he was going to be paralyzed after he recovered.

On the day of Mikey's funeral, Reggie was still in the hospital so Lil J and the rest of his guys had to go without him.

The wake was held at the funeral home on 159th street in Harvey. Everybody was there from Mikey's family and all of the women that he had been with throughout the course of his life to all of the real street niggas. Even some of the fake ass niggas showed up like they were trying to pay their respects when really all they were trying to do was come up on a bitch.

While the pastor was giving the eulogy, Rick and Dollicia walked into the funeral home. Lil J was up in front with Mikey's family so he didn't notice them until they walked up to Mikey's closed casket.

This bitch ass nigga must think shit sweet! Lil J thought. He wanted to get up and put a few bullets inside Rick's head, but maintained his cool because the time and place wasn't right.

After the pastor finished saying the eulogy, and everybody was leaving the funeral home getting ready to go to the burial site, Lil J and his guys fell back to try to console Mikey's grieving family when all of a sudden Lil' J's phone was alerted by J. J.

"Yo." Lil J hollered through this chirp.

"The police on location, and they deep as hell!" J. J hollered back. Him and Ant were outside posted inside of a minivan with two AR-15s. Zed had told them to watch the area just in case the niggas from Robbins decided to show up.

"Damn! What they on?"

"I don't know but they coming ya'll way."

When Lil J turned around and looked at the door, he saw Detective Bradly, Jones, and about eight other detectives flood the funeral home with guns drawn.

"What's up Lil J? What it is?" K. B asked ready to pull his guns and get it on.

Lil J looked over to Mikey's sister before he spoke. "Stand down Lil bruh. This ain't the time or the place for that."

"What about the heat we holding?"

"Minor gun cases. Two to five. Three to seven at the most. It ain't worth it."

"John Leebo, I'm taking you and your boys in." Detective Bradly said as he approached Lil J.

"For what?"

"I don't know yet, but we'll think of something once we get you all down to the station."

"Aarrgh!" Lil J winced in pain as Detective Bradly slapped the handcuffs on him.

"You in a little pain? What…you got hurt at the liquor store?"

"You just gone come in here and disrespect my man funeral like this?"

"Fuck yo man, he got what he deserved. And what's this?" Detective Bradly said as he pulled a .45 Ruger out of Lil J's pocket.

"I knew you were holding."

"Shit, the rest of these niggas holding too." said Detective Jones. Him and the other detectives had handcuffed and searched the rest of Lil J's crew.

"Good, now let's take these dumb mu'tha fuckas' in."

☙

Across the street from the funeral home at the gas station, Wayne was inside of a Yukon with Greg. They had watched the police raid the funeral home but thought nothing of it because all Wayne was trying to do was show Greg who Lil J was.

"Ay, which one of them niggas is the target?" Greg asked as he watched the police bring Lil J and his guys out of the funeral home in handcuffs.

Damn, I wonder what they locking them up for? Wayne thought. Somebody must be talking. "The short cat who they putting in the back of that squad car that just pulled up."

"You think the police locking them up for that other shit you told me about?"

"I don't know, but I need to find out." Wayne said before he put the truck in drive and pulled off.

☙

Inside of the Harvey police station, Lil J was in a cell laying on his back staring at the ceiling. Him and his guys were locked in different holding cells and the only way that they could communicate with each other was through a chuckhole inside of the doors.

Earlier when Lil J and his guys were brought into the police station, they were taken into the interrogation room one by one and was interrogated by Detective Bradly and Jones about the incident that occurred at the liquor store. After a few hours of getting nowhere, Detective Bradly decided to leave them in lockup overnight. He knew that he could only hold them for forty eight hours, so he was planning on coming back in the morning and picking up where him and Jones left off.

While Lil J was still staring at the ceiling thinking about all of the things that had transpired since he came home, the beautiful goddess that came to Mikey's funeral with Rick popped back into his head. He had made a mental note back at the funeral home to ask his guys who she was, but when the police locked him up he forgot all about it until now; so he decided to go to the chuckhole and ask Zed who she was. "Yo Zed." he hollered.

Silence

"Zed". He hollered again.

"I think that nigga sleep." X said as he came to the chuckhole.

"X."

"What up?"

"What you on over there?"

"Shit man, I'm hoping these bitches don't charge us with them bangers."

"Don't sweat that shit man cause if they do we just gone bond out."

"I ain't gone be able to bond out because I'm already on probation. And I know I'ma have a hold on whatever bond they give me until I go before my probation judge."

"What you on probation for?"

"Some fucking guns that I got popped with out in the Rezzo's on some drunk shit last year."

"That's crazy, but don't trip on that shit."

"What you was calling Zed for?" X asked changing the subject.

"Aw damn, I almost forgot. You remember shorty that came to the funeral with Rick – right?"

"Yeah, what about her?"

"Who was she?"

"She dude main bitch, but she fuck with hoes tho."

"Yeah?" Lil J said as he began pondering."What's her name?" He asked.

"Dollicia."

"Zed and Reggie was telling me about her at the pancake house about a week and a half ago. They told me that she was bad, but I didn't think she was that mu'fuck'n bad."

"Yeah, that hoe is bad, but I don't think she gone step out on dude." X said already knowing what Lil J was thinking.

Lil J laughed. "I ain't on that bruh, but I'm 'bout to fall back. I'ma get up with you in the morning." he said before he went back to his bunk and laid down.

Detective Bradly and Jones made it back to the police station around four o'clock the next day. When they took Lil J and his guys back into the interrogation room and got the same results as they did the day before, they decided to just charge them with the guns.

Lil J knew that him and his guys were going to have to wait until they went before the judge in the morning to get a bond, so when he got his phone call he called Linzy and told her to come to court in the morning with some bond money.

※

Out in Midlothian at the One Stop Insurance Agency, Beautyful was sitting in front of the computer thinking about Lil J. She was trying to figure out why he hadn't returned any of her calls. Every time she called his phone it went straight to voicemail, so she left him three messages in hopes that he would eventually check them and give her a call. But two days had passed since then and she was becoming angered that he still hadn't called.

I knew I shouldn't have started liking that damn boy. He probably out with some –

"Beautyful, go pull Robert Lipscomb's file for me." Fannie hollered from her office.

Beautyful exhaled a deep breath. *Won't you get up and get it yoself.*

"Beautyful, did you hear me?"

"Yes, I'm getting it now." Beautyful said as she got up and went to the file cabinet. After she found the file and took it to Fannie, her phone started vibrating on her hip. When she looked at the caller I. D. and saw Lil J's number, she became filled with excitement. "Hello." She answered.

"What's up baby girl?"

"Don't you what's up baby girl me. Where you been? And why haven't you returned any of my calls?"

"Whoa, slow down baby. Don't kill me."

"Answer my questions."

"Some bullshit happened the other day B, but that's neither here nor there. I called you to let you know that I'm 'bout to go out of town."

"You just disappeared for two days, and now you talking about going out of town. How long do you plan on being gone?"

"I don't know, probably about a week or two. I'm going out to Miami tho."

"And you telling me this because?"

"Beautyful, I know you smart enough to read between the lines." Lil J said as he paused for a brief moment. "I want you to come with me."

A smile spread across Beautyful's face. "I don't have any money to go out of town with you."

"You don't need none, I got you."

"What we gone do when we get out there?"

"Whatever you wanna do, but I just wanna chill."

"So you about to go all the way out to Miami just to chill?"

"Yeah, I'm just try'na get away from this bullshit for awhile."

"When are we leaving?"

Lil J looked at the time on his phone. "It's three now so I'm gone call the travel agency after I get off the phone with you and book us a Villa at one of the resorts down in South Beach. I'm trying to leave tonight after you get off work, so I'ma get us some first class tickets too."

"Tonight! I need to get – "

"Beautyful, what I tell you about talking on that damn phone inside of my office!" Fannie snapped as she came out of her back office.

"Oh shit, my boss tripping. I'm gone talk to you later." Beautyful whispered into the phone.

"I'ma meet you at yo apartment at eight, so try'da leave work early."

"Okay bye." She said before ending the call. She was excited that Lil J was taking her out of town with him, but she was skeptical about leaving so soon. She needed to get her hair and nails done plus come up with something to tell her boss so that she could at least get a week off. Maybe she could tell her boss that she had a death in the family. Whatever she was going to do she had about five hours to think about it.

☙

While Lil J was getting ready to go out of town, Greg was riding around doing research on him; and some of the things that he found out was confusing. Greg had found out that Lil J's real name was John Leebo, and that he had moved to Harvey from Chicago Heights when he was younger.

Greg had an ex-crack head auntie that used to live in Chicago Heights back in the '90s. And he remembered that she had a son named John that she sent to Harvey. But the thing that had him confused was that he didn't know whether or not the John that he was paid to eliminate was his little cousin or not. And he didn't want to go through with the hit and find out later that it was his cousin, so he headed out to Homewood to his Aunt Ruth's house. He had been over there many times while dropping his mother off and picking her up, but he had never been inside.

"Gregory?" Ruth asked after she opened her front door. She was surprised to see him without his mother and began wondering if something was wrong.

"Yeah, how you doing auntie?"

"I'm okay, but is there something wrong?"

"Nah ain't nothing wrong. I just stopped by because I needed to talk to you."

"Well come on in then." Ruth said as she opened the door a little wider and stepped aside.

"Do you want some tea or coffee or anything?"

"Nah I'm cool." Greg said as he walked through the door and into her living room. When he sat down on the couch he noticed a portrait hanging on the wall just above the TV. The portrait was a sketch of Ruth and a guy that looked identical to the guy that he saw the police bring out of the funeral home.

"So what is it that you need to talk to me about?" Ruth asked as she walked into the living room and sat down across from Greg.

"Auntie, who is that guy in that picture standing next to you?"

Ruth looked at the portrait before she spoke. "That's my son John. You don't remember him?"

"Not really. The last time I seen him was three months before you sent him to Harvey when we were younger."

"Sending my baby away was the hardest thing that I've ever had to do. But it was either that or let him get lost in the system like me and my sisters did, and I just couldn't bear those thought." Ruth said before falling silent.

Greg saw the pain in his auntie's eyes and knew that he had brought back memories that should have never been revived. His aunt had been clean from drugs for seven years now and he was proud of her. She had a beautiful well furnished house and a nice Cadillac that she cherished, and she went to Church faithfully.

Greg wanted to tell her about the guys that were after her son, but didn't want to scare or bring her any more sorrow, so he just got Lil J's number from her and left.

CHAPTER 19

When Beautyful made it to the Vail apartments and parked her car, an Infiniti truck pulled up behind her. Ten seconds later her phone started going off.

"Hello." She answered.

"You twenty minutes late. What took you so long?" Lil J asked.

"My boss wouldn't let me leave early, but she gave me a week off."

"Good, now come on and let's ride."

"About that – "

"Aw shit, don't tell me that you change yo mind."

"Naw, I ain't change my mind."

"Let's ride then baby girl."

Beautyful fell silent for a minute before she spoke. "I need my hair and nails done, and I need to go shopping." She pouted.

Lil J laughed. "You sound like a big 'ol baby. I'll take you to do all that stuff out in Miami tomorrow. Now let's ride before we miss our flight."

"Alright, let me run up to my apartment and grab a few things real quick."

"Hurry up." Lil J said before ending the call.

Four and a half hours later Lil J and Beautyful were inside of their villa out in one of Miami, Florida's marvelous resorts. The villa that they stayed in had two bedrooms that both contained 5' x 7' sunken whirlpool tubs, cozy fireplaces and massage chairs. The villa also had a patio with an adjacent court yard.

After Beautyful finished admiring the villa, she grabbed her things and went into one of the bedrooms. Lil J thought about being in the same room with her, but disregarded the thought and took the other room because he didn't want her to feel uncomfortable; plus he had a lot on his mind and needed time to sort through this problems.

The eight hours that Beautyful put in at work, plus the plane ride had her so exhausted that she stripped down to her pajamas and plopped down on the king sized bed as soon as she got into the room. She tried to stay up to see if Lil J was going to come get in the bed with her but she dozed off after five minutes.

When she woke up the next morning, she was surprised to see that she was still alone, so after she took care of her hygiene she went into the other room and found Lil J sound asleep. As she walked closer to the bed she admired how handsome and relaxed he looked while he slept.

"What's wrong B?" Lil J asked after he opened his eyes and saw Beautyful staring at him.

"Nothing." Beautyful replied before she sat down on the bed next to him.

"What time is it?"

"Almost eleven."

"You ready to go shopping?"

Beautyful nodded her head. "I'm ready whenever you are."

"Aight, give me a minute to take care of – "

"Oh my God!" Beautyful exclaimed when she saw the bandage on Lil J's shoulder after he moved the covers and raised up.

"What! What! What's wrong?" Lil J asked, wondering what she was getting so frantic about.

"Your shoulder; what happened to you?"

Lil J laughed. "Girl you got me thinking that something wrong for real, this ain't shit. I got shot in the shoulder last week."

"It ain't shit? You say that like it's just a paper cut or something."

Lil J gave Beautyful a cold stare before he responded. "One of my guys lost his life the night I got shot. And another one got shot-up so bad that he may never be able to walk again. I caught a blessing to be sitting here talking to you with only a hole in my shoulder that's really not affecting me" he said before he got up and walked into the washroom to take care of his number one.

While Lil J was in the washroom taking care of his B. I. Beautyful remained seated on the bed lost in wonder. She was having negative thoughts about the street life that Lil J was mixed up in and was hoping that it didn't become the cause of her getting hurt in the near future.

While Beautyful was still dealing with her thoughts, Lil J walked back into the room and interrupted them.

"B, I need you to change these bandages for me." He said as he grabbed his first aid kit and handed it to her before he sat down.

Beautyful got up and pulled the old bandages off him before she dug into the bag and pulled out the new ones. "Aren't you about tired of the streets after everything that you've been through?"

"Hell yeah I am."

"So why don't you just leave 'em alone then?" she asked as she began cleaning his wounds.

"Because it ain't that simple."

"It's just as simple as this vacation that we out here on. All you have to do is leave and don't go back.

"Everything I got and worked hard for is out there, plus the people I love."

"You could take the people that you love with you. And if the things that you got and worked hard for is material, then they can always be replaced. Your life is more important." Beautyful said before she paused. "Lil J, going to jail then coming home and getting shot should show you that the streets are not worth it."

"Is you done yet B?" Lil J asked, not really wanting to hear anymore of the lecture that she was giving him even though he knew that she was right.

"Excuse me!" Beautyful retorted with an incredulous look on her face.

Lil J smiled. "I'm talking about with the bandages."

"Aw, hold on." Beautyful said before she applied the last piece of tape to his bandages. "Okay, I'm finished."

Good. Lil J thought before he got up and threw his shirt on. I'ma 'bout to call down to the chef and get us some breakfast sent up here before we leave." He said as he picked up the phone and dialed the kitchen.

Ten minutes after Lil J and Beautyful finished eating, they headed over to Ocean Drive and shopped until about three o'clock. Lil J had already spent over ten grand on Beautyful by buying her everything that she wanted and everything that he thought looked good on her, and he was about ready to call it a day.

"B, I'm tired of running around out here, let's go back to the villa and get a massage or something." Lil J said as him and Beautyful were walking out of a jewelry store. He had just dropped eleven hundred on a white gold bracelet that he thought looked good on her and she couldn't stop admiring it.

"What about my hair and nails?" Beautyful asked as she managed to pull her attention away from the bracelet.

"You can get that stuff done tomorrow cant' you?"

"Naw, I wanna get it done today."

"Aight, you gone have to go by yoself cause my shoulder starting to hurt."

"You know I don't know how to get to the hair salon or the nail shop." Beautyful said as she folded her arms.

"B, after you drop me off all you gotta do is use the Onstar to get over to Collins. The nail shop and hair salon is on Collins, so you shouldn't have no problem finding them."

"You sure know a lot about out here. What, you brought one of yo hood rats out here before?"

Lil J chuckled and shook his head. "I got a few homies from the A that come out here all the time." He said before handing the valet his ticket.

"So you're not gonna go with me?"

"I told you that my shoulder hurting and I'm tired of being out here. If you wait until tomorrow I'll go with you."

"Naw…I don't wanna wait until tomorrow. I'm going today, but I see that you're not a man of your words."

Lil J cracked a smile. Beautyful was smarter than what he gave her credit for. She knew exactly what to do to get what she wanted. "And what were my words?"

"Your exact words were, I'll take you to do all that stuff out in Miami tomorrow."

"Photographic memory huh? And those were my words?"

"Yes, those were your words."

"Well, I guess I gotta stand by 'em then. Let's ride." Lil J said as the valet pulled up with their rental car.

☙

Back out in Harvey, Rick, Wayne and Calvin were in the back of Calvin's barber shop holding a meeting.

"I' ma 'bout to fly out to the Bahamas for a couple weeks so I'ma need ya'll to keep shit in order while I'm gone." Rick said as he paused. He had gone to see his uncle Ron earlier in the day and got grilled about the shit that happened to Lil J and his guys.

Ron wasn't so much tripping about Lil J getting shot or losing his guys. He was tripping on Rick for letting the shit that happened transpire right after Lil J left his club, knowing that it was a possibility that the shit could be traced back to him.

"Calvin, I want you to keep doing what you've been doing and keep shit right on the business side. Wayne, I want you to stay in touch with Tank and Greg and make sure that they on top of business. Matter fact, what that nigga Tank been on so far anyway?"

"Bullshit, him and his guys been riding through Lil J's hood even tho' I told they ass that the nigga gone out of town. They on some thirsty shit tho', so I'm suspecting that they gone fuck up and be dead or in jail sooner than later."

"What they be on when they be riding through dude shit?"

"Ain't no telling, but dude ain't out there, so whatever they be doing is meaningless."

"So in other words, they ain't doing shit but bring unnecessary heat and attention to their selves."

"Basically."

Rick shook his head. "Tank always doing redundant ass shit. That's the only boss I know that acts like a soldier. But anyway, what's up with Greg? Is he progressing or just wasting my fucking money?"

"He still doing his research, but he claim he got this shit in the bag."

"Well tell him to hurry that shit up because I want that nigga done before I come back."

"When you leaving?"

"In the morning. I was suppose to leave tonight but my girl and her new girlfriend wanna have some fun. And ya'll know I'm always down to have some fun with my girl and her girlfriends." Rick said before cracking a smile.

&

When Lil J made it over to Collins and pulled up to a spa resort, Beautyful began protesting.

"This is a spa, what are we doing here?" she asked.

"This ain't just a spa. They do nails in here too. But I came here because I wanna get a massage while you getting yo nails done."

"I'm not about to let you get a massage without me." Beautyful said before grabbing his hand and locking her fingers between his.

"So what, I'm suppose to sit around here and look stupid until you finish getting yo nails done?"

Beautyful laughed. "Naw silly. You gone get a manicure or a pedicure."

"Aight let's just hurry up." Lil J said as he agreed. When he started getting his manicure he couldn't help but to admire all of the beautiful women around him. He cursed hisself for bringing Beautyful instead of his guys because some of the women were giving him flirtatious stares letting him know that they were digging him.

After Lil J and Beautyful were finished getting their nails done, they were escorted to one of the back rooms where the masseuses came and started their massages.

Lil J was enjoying the massage and became so relaxed that he dozed off. When he opened his eyes he was no longer at the spa resort, and Beautyful was no longer beside him. He was inside of a big, luxurious room laying in a king size bed receiving some good brain from Brittney, one of the kissing cousins.

Marquisha and some other women were laying down right next to them in a sixty nine position feasting on each other.

While Brittney continued doing her thing with the head game Lil J was enjoying every second of it until the other women pulled her head from between Marquisha's legs.

"Dollicia!" Lil J blurted out as she began crawling towards him. The lust in her eyes had him excited and he wanted to feel hisself inside of her so bad that he pulled his dick out of Brittney's mouth and let Dollicia straddle him.

So this what it is huh? Lil J thought as Dollicia eased her pussy down on his shaft. She made sure that she felt every inch of him inside of her before she began popping her pussy on his dick.

Aw hell yeah. He said to hisself as he lifted his head up and watched his dick go in and out of Dollicia's fat pussy.

Dollicia had some damn good pussy and Lil J was enjoying it so much that he stopped focusing on everything except for her, and that was a mistake that he would soon regret because as soon as he exploded inside of her, Rick, Tank and Mack busted inside of the room with big guns drawn.

Lil J reached under his pillow and became sick to his stomach once he came up empty handed.

Dollicia was still on top of Lil J but didn't feel his dick anymore because he had gone soft. After she got up and walked over to Rick and kissed him on the mouth, Lil J knew that fucking with her was a mistake that had cost him his life.

"Dirty bitches." Lil J said as he watched Mack kill Brittney and Marquisha.

"Lil J, it looks like yo road has come to an end, but it is what it is." Rick said before giving Tank the green light.

Tank trained his AK on Lil J and let it ride. The first slug caught him in his right shoulder and knocked his whole arm off.

"Aagghhh!" Lil J hollered as he woke up in pain.

"What happened? What's wrong?" Beautyful asked as she jumped up.

"I'm sorry! I'm sorry! Please forgive me!" the masseuse said in a frantic tone of voice.

"Don't worry about it, its okay." Lil J said relieved that he was only dreaming.

"What the hell happened!" Beautyful snapped wanting to know what the hell was going on.

"I – I accidentally put too much pressure on his shoulder." The masseuse said.

"B, calm down. It wasn't as serious as it sounded."

"You sure? Because we can leave and go get my hair done and finish getting massages back at the villa."

"Yeah, I'm sho', but we can still leave, let's ride."

CHAPTER 20

Back in the hood over on 159th in Lexington, Zed, Zep and K.B were in one of their armory spots with Terry and T.Y loading up choppers and putting on bullet proof vests. They were getting ready to take Terry and T.Y out to the old projects and let them scope'em out.

Terry and T.Y were two young hitters that Zed had holding down the buildings that they were at. He didn't plan on getting it cracking while they were with him, but he was making sure that he was prepared just in case something went wrong.

"Terry, remember, all I want ya'll to do is walk to the end of the projects, then turn around and walk back the same way ya'll came. Be very observant tho' look for niggas in cuts, niggas on top of roofs, and anything else that might help." Said Zed.

"You want us to take our guns with us?" T.Y inquired.

"Nah, because nine times out of ten ya'll gone be stopped, either on ya'll way going through there, or coming back. And if they search ya'll and find guns, they gone take 'em or try'da get down on ya'll.

"What we suppose to tell them if they stop us?" Terry inquired.

"Tell they ass that ya'll looking for some weed. Let 'em know that ya'll looking for some weed; and that ya'll ain't from out here, ya'll from Texas, and ya'll cousin told ya'll that it was a weed spot in the projects somewhere."

"Zed, you don't think they gone fuck up do you?" K.B inquired.

"Hell nah, it's too simple, but we gone be on point anyway."

"When we gone go through there and get shit cracking?"

"As soon as J get back."

"You heard from him yet?"

"Nah, but he should be hitting me up soon." Zed said as he threw his shirt on over his vest. "Grab them guns and let's ride tho."

☙

When Lil J and Beautyful made it back to their villa, Lil J dipped off into his room and took off his shirt before he started counting the rest of his money. He had brought thirty thousand with him and had spent close to twenty thousand already and was wondering if he was going to need some more wired to him.

After he finished counting his money, he picked up his phone and called Zed.

"What's up bruh? What it is?" Zed asked after picking up on the second ring.

"Shit man, I'm out here spending all my money on shorty ass."

"Aw you trick'n?"

"Yeah man, but you know what they say; it ain't trick'n if you got it."

"Right, right, but what's up with that shoulder? How's it feeling?"

"It's still kina sore, but it should be good in about another week." Lil J said as he rotated his arm.

"Good, cuz mu'fuckas ready to get it cracking."

"Speaking of getting it cracking. I dozed off at the spa earlier and had this wild ass dream about that bitch Dollicia." Lil J said as his phone beeped letting him know that somebody was trying to call him on his other line.

"That dream must've been exclusive."

"Exclusive! Shit, that bitch had me set-up, but somebody hitting my other line so I'ma have to tell you about it later."

"Just hit me back."

"Aight." Lil J said before he clicked over. "Who this is?" he asked.

"This Greg man. What's happening?"

"Greg…..Fuck I know you from?"

"I'm yo cousin nigga."

"I ain't got no mu'fuckin' cousin name Greg."

"Man this Gregory; C.C son. You don't remember me?"

"Aw yeah, I remember you nigga. I ain't heard from yo ass in so long, I damn near forgot about you, but what's happening tho'?"

"I need to holler at you about some serious shit. That's what's happen'n."

This nigga must've heard that I'm that nigga, and wanna come fuck with me. "Aight, I'm listening."

"Not over the phone."

"Well it's gone have to wait because I'm all the way at the bottom of the map right now." Lil J said as the lights in his room dimmed.

He heard a melody coming from the speakers but really couldn't place the song.

When he looked around to see what the hell was going on, he saw Beautyful standing in the doorway in some all white lingerie looking like a goddess.

Goddamn! He said to himself, as Johnny Gill flooded the villa.

♫ **Girl you are so fine/I can't believe my eyes.** ♫

"Cuz, what the fuck going on?" Greg asked. He had been talking to Lil J for the last few seconds and wasn't getting any response.

"Nothing cuz, but something just come up. I'ma hit yo phone when I get back to the hood tho'," Lil J said as he ended the call before kicking off his shoes and leaning back in the bed.

Beautyful had made her way over to the king size bed and was crawling towards Lil J. When she finally made it to him she began gently kissing his lips.

OOhh she a fool for this White Diamond, he thought as he inhaled Beautyful's perfume. When he lifted his back up off the bed and was about to roll her onto her back so that he could take over, she stopped him by putting her hand on his chest and shaking her head. "I got this." she said before she went down and started planting kisses on his chest.

When she made it down to his navel she stopped and unfastened his pants before pulling his dick out. *This nigga holding.* she thought as she moistened up her mouth and started licking up and down his shaft. Once she had it nice and lubed she took him into her mouth and started bobbing slowly.

Aw yeah, now this what it is. Lil J thought as Beautyful started taking care of good business with her head game. It wasn't as good as Brittney's, but he was enjoying it.

When Beautyful looked up and saw that he was laid back looking too relaxed, she pulled him out of her mouth and started making him go crazy by sucking and rolling her tongue around the head of his dick at the same time.

Damn! I though they said she was a good girl. she a mu'fuck'n undercover freak. Lil J thought as he tried to place his hand on top of her head.

"Uh-Uh." She said as she reached up and blocked his hand. After she felt that she had teased him enough she pulled him back into her mouth and started back bobbing.

"OH SHIT!" Lil J blurted, as he tried to contain himself.

Aw I got this nigga. Beautyful thought. She knew that Lil J was about to cum from the way that he was squirming, so she picked up the pace and started bobbing just a little faster.

"Aaahhh!" Lil J hollered as he exploded inside of her mouth.

Beautyful stopped bobbing but kept her lips locked around the head of Lil J's dick. Once she knew that he was done nutting she pulled him completely out of her mouth and went into the washroom.

Man, baby girl would'a had Brittney faded if she would'a swallowed and kept going. Lil J thought as he was laid back trying to regain his composure.

"John, I'ma 'bout to use some of your mouth wash."

"Gone 'head." Lil J said before he rose up and took a few aspirins. He was about to show Beautyful just how much of a beast he was and didn't want no interruptions from his shoulder.

When Beautyful came out of the washroom, Lil J got up and stripped her of her lingerie before laying her in the bed.

She take care of this mu'fucker. Lil J thought after he spread Beautyful's legs and admired her evenly shaved pussy before he went down and began feasting.

"Ooh yeah. Just like that." Beautyful said as she began moaning.

Lil J had started off by licking all over Beautyful's pearl tongue, but when her moans started turning him on he began sucking and licking simultaneously, making her moan even louder.

Beautyful's moans were like music to Lil J's ears, so he decided to take things up a notch. He inserted two of his fingers inside of her and began working her love tunnel.

"Unh…OH…Johnnn.." Beautyful moaned as she came hard.

This girl ain't never cum already. Lil J thought before he pulled his fingers out of her and went down and began devouring her juices.

After he finished eating from Beautyful's love tunnel, he rose up and climbed between her legs before sliding inside of her.

"Ah." Beautyful moaned as she reached her arms out and grabbed Lil J. She hadn't had sex in two years and it felt as if his dick was ripping her walls apart.

Damn this pussy tight. Lil J thought as he slid the rest of his dick inside of Beautyful before he began long stroking her. When she began moaning he started stroking deeper. He was getting turned on more and more from the seductive fuck faces that she made every time he thrust inside of her.

When he pulled her legs up and started thrusting deeper, she came causing him to shoot his load all inside of her.

I love this girl already. Lil J said to himself as he stayed on top of Beautyful with his dick inside of her for a whole three minutes.

I hope he don't think it's over. Beautyful said to herself as she felt Lil J going soft inside of her. When he pulled out of her and rolled over, she rose up and played with his dick until it stood back up before she straddled him and began riding.

Lil J had regained his composure and was enjoying the ride so much that he reached his hands out and gripped Beautyful's ass cheeks and started helping her bounce her pussy on his dick.

Beautyful was feeling Lil J's dick all up in her stomach, and it was feeling so good that when she came her body went limp and she lost her composure.

"Whoa, what the hell!" Lil J said as he caught Beautyful. She had leaned so hard to the side that she almost fell.

"What's wrong B?"

"Nothin'." She moaned shaking her head as Lil J laid her down.

"You came while you was up there?"

She nodded slowly.

"Well I didn't. Turnover and let me hit it from the back." He said as he helped Beautyful rise up and turn around before he slid inside of her and began pounding.

"Unh...Unh...Oh...." Beautyful moaned.

It was something about the way that she moaned that just turned Lil J the hell on. So every time she moaned he pounded harder. He continued to pound, thrusting in and out of her until they both came together for the last time that night.

Throughout the remainder of their vacation, Lil J took Beautyful to Disney World, Universal Studios and Paradise Island. When it was finally over with and time for them to head back out to the Midwest, they weren't ready to go. They wanted to stay at Paradise Island forever, but they knew that it wasn't happening. Beautyful had to get back because Fannie only gave her a week off. She had caught feeling for Lil J and was hoping that she made the right decision by letting him into her life. She was also hoping that she could somehow cajole him into leaving the streets alone and moving to Georgia with her.

Lil J had to get back too because he missed his son, and he had a lot of unfinished business to attend to, plus his guys needed him. The vacation with Beautyful was something that he really needed because it relieved him of a lot of stress and tension. He had fallen for Beautyful, and really wanted to fuck with her, but he had to sort out his problems in the hood first. The storm was about to come, and he knew that it was a possibility that he wouldn't make it through it. So he chose not to count his eggs before they hatched, and planned on taking things one step at a time.

But if things did go right and he lived through the storm, he planned on getting his son and leaving the hood. And if things were still good with Beautyful, he'd take her with them too.

CHAPTER 21

When Lil J and Beautyful made it back to Chicago, Zed was waiting for them at the airport in a rental car. After they dropped Beautyful off at her apartment, they headed to the hospital to see Reggie. While they were riding, Zed broke the silence.

"So J, what's to shorty?"

"A beast." Lil J said anticipating the question. "I think I'm in love."

"Damn, it's like that?"

"Hell yeah. She got a bomb bomb."

"Aw you gone have to set that shit out then."

"I'll have to kill you."

"That's how you feel?"

"I told you I think I'm in love."

Zed laughed. "Yo soft ass."

"Fuck you."

"Nah, fuck her, but anyway while you was out of town playing Romeo and Juliet, I was out in Robbins getting the ins, outs, ups and downs of the projects, and me and the guys ready to go through there whenever you ready."

"Shit, we can ride through there tonight if you got everything mapped out. But tell me how it's looking over there."

"It's kinda tight. Tank, Mack and Rob holding shit down over there and our main focus is on them. But they got a lot of young shooters over there that might get in our way, so we gone take J.J, Ant and a few shorties from our other block over there with us and let them chop shit up while we hit the spots where Tank, and them be at."

"Aight we can do it like that, but we might not need J. J. and them. I talked to my man Lunitic yesterday and he told me that he was gone bring a few of his goons out here and get shit cracking with us whenever we ready."

"What about X?" We ain't gone wait on him to get out?"

"Not if Lunitic and his guys show up, but if they don't then we might have to wait." Lil J said as they pulled up to the hospital.

After Zed parked the car, him and Lil J made their way into the hospital. When they got up to Reggie's room, they saw that he was laid back talking on the phone looking like a werewolf.

Damn my boy look bad. Lil J thought as him and Zed walked over and showed Reggie some love. "What's up jo? What's good?"

Reggie ended his phone call before he spoke. "You tell me what's good nigga. I heard you took Beautyful out of town."

Reggie was pissed off about his situation, but he was optimistic so he didn't trip, cry, or complain about it. He had a good run in the streets and was still alive, unlike his main man Mikey who he missed dearly.

"Yeah I did, but it wasn't shit tho'."

Reggie gave Lil J a dubious look. "Man knock it the fuck off and tell me what was to that shit."

Lil J smiled. "She got the bomb."

"I knew it! I fucking knew it!" Reggie hollered. "That bitch look like she go that fire."

"That bitch got good brain too."

"Yeah, is she better than Brittney?"

"Hell nah, she up there tho'. But speaking of Brittney, I had a wild ass dream about that bitch and her friend while I was out there." Lil J said as he started telling them the story of his dream. When he was finished he saw that they had caught on to what he was really getting at.

"So let me guess, you gone use Brittney and Marquisha to get close to Dollicia so that they could set Rick up the way that you was set-up in yo dream?" Reggie asked.

"Bingo."

"Ain't gone happen."

"What you mean?" Lil J looked addled.

"That bitch mad as hell at you for ducking her. She text my phone the other day cursing you out. She say she don't ever want to see you again."

"Man give me that bitch number. I got the gift of gab."

"Aight, but let's say you do get back in good with the bitch. How is you gone convince her to go through with the set-up?"

"That's gone be the easy part. I'ma promise the bitch a fortune that she ain't gone live to see." Lil J said as he smiled.

"I forgot to tell you. That nigga Rick went out of town the other day." Said Zed.

"Fuck he go?" Lil J mugged his face up.

"Shit, I don't know."

"Did his bitch go with him?"

"Nah."

"Aight, that's good. Brittney a have some time to get acquainted with her while he ain't around." Lil J said as his phone started going off.

"What up?" he answered.

"Ay Lil cuz, what it is?" Greg asked.

"Shit, I'm just getting back, but what's good?"

"You ain't forgot that I need to rotate with you right?"

"Nah, I ain't forgot, but I'm at the hospital kicking it with my man right now."

"Just hit my phone whenever you leave."

"I got you." Lil J said before ending the call.

"Who the fuck was that?" Zed asked.

"My cousin Greg."

Zed frowned his face up. "Greg, you ain't never told me you had a cousin name Greg."

"I ain't never told you about him because I forgot about him."

"What's up with Zep and K.B What they on?" Reggie asked, changing the subject.

"I got them niggas out in Robbins keeping an eye on the projects." Said Zed.

"Damn, I almost forgot to call Lunitic." Lil J said before he grabbed his phone and called Lunitic.

"What up bruh?" Lunitic answered on the second ring. "You niggas ready yet?"

"Yeah, you coming through?"

"Yeah, I'll be out there in a minute."

"Hit me when you get off the E-way."

"Aight." Lunitic said before ending the call.

"What you niggas 'bout to get on?" Reggie asked, kind of in the dark to what was going on.

Lil J lowered his voice. "We about to go burn them bitches in the projects."

"What? Zed I thought you said going through the projects was like a suicide mission."

"It is, but it's about time we showed them bitch ass niggas that we ain't scared to come through there." said Zed.

"So it's a chance that some of ya'll might not make it back?"

"Reggie, you talking like we don't take these same chances in the hood daily."

"What about X?"

"That nigga don't go back to court until next week, so we just gone take care of this shit without him." said Lil J.

Reggie shook his head. "Just be careful out there."

"We will, we gone have some goons from Lunitic hood out there with us too, so we should be good." Lil J said as they continued to kick it until Lunitic called his phone.

～

"Mack, go get all the guys together. I'm tired of waiting for this bitch ass nigga!" Tank hollered before he downed the rest of the Hennessy that he was drinking. Him and his guys had been riding through Lil J's block every day since the incident at the liquor store and were becoming very impatient.

They had planned on catching Lil J at the funeral home, but the police had beat them to the punch, and now Lil J was gone out of town.

"If dude ain't back when we ride through there this time, we gone shoot his block up and burn his buildings down."

"Who all we taking out there with us?" Mack inquired.

"All the hitters."

"I thought you said – "

"Go do what the fuck I said and stop asking so many questions!" Tank snapped as he got up and stumbled before catching his balance. He was so blotto to the point where Mack started doubting his judgment, but it was his call so Mack went and did as he was told. Five minutes later he had twelve young riders ready to roll.

"You let them niggas know what the business was?"

"Yeah, they know what it is." said Mack.

"Let's ride then."

☙

"What the fuck they on? K.B,You see this shit?" Zep inquired.

"How the fuck am I suppose to see some shit when you got the binoculars?" K. B. asked, mugged up.

"These niggas on some shit. They deep as hell." Zep said as he watched Tank and his guys hop in their whips and pull out of the projects.

"They probably about to ride through our hood like they been doing for the last week."

"Zed need to gone and ok it so we can toast these bitches." Zep said as he grabbed his phone.

"Now you talking." K.B said as he started the car up and threw it in drive before he pulled out of the cut and caught up with Tank's Entourage.

"Yo." Zed hollered through his chirp after Zep alerted his phone.

"These niggas on the move, and they deep as hell."

"Which way they headed?"

"Towards the hood."

"We in the hood."

"Well be on point then because they headed ya'll way."

☙

When Zed got the chirp from Zep, he was at the Vail apartment buildings along with Lil J, Lunitic and Lunitic's guys. They were all inside of the armory picking over hand guns and choppers.

"Ay, my Lil brother said them niggas just left the projects. They might be on their way over here so hurry up and grab what ya'll need."

"Zed, hit Zep back and see how many cars them niggas rolling in." Lil J said before he pulled his phone out of his pocket and hollered through his chirp. "J. J."

"What up?"

"I want you and Ant to go post up in the cut on 148th and be on point."

"Aight." Came back through the chirp.

"Zep said them niggas in four cars and a van." said Zed.

"How many niggas coming?" One of Lunitic's guys asked.

"I don't know, but my Lil brother say they deep."

"Fuck how deep they is, let's just go out here and wait on them bitches." Lunitic said as he tucked his D-eagle along with a .40 in his waist band before picking up an AK-47. The rest of his guys preferred AR-15s, Mac 11's and SKS's.

Lil J and Zed both picked up AR-15s after stuffing a few hand guns.

When they made it outside, Lil J looked up to the balcony and shook his head when he saw Mal and B posted with choppers. They weren't killers, they were money getters, but it was good to see that they were standing firm.

"Zed, I got J. J and – "

"Yo," Zep's voice came through Zed's phone and cut Lil J off.

"What up?" Zed hollered back.

"These niggas splitting up, and they coming ya'll way."

"Aight." Zed hollered back through his chirp. "Ya'll heard him, right?"

"Yeah." said Lil J. "I got J. J and Ant at 148th, take B and Mal and watch the front.

Me and Tic got the back." Lil J said before they split.

☙

Tank was sitting on the passenger side of the Chevy van that Mack was driving so drunk that Mack started thinking that going through Lil J's hood was a bad idea.

"Tank, what' up jo? We almost there." Mack said as they were approaching the light on 147th on Dixie highway.

Tank raised up from his reclined seat and looked out the window before he spoke.

"Rob, chirp B.C. and Gary and tell them to turn off right here and come around – "

"Tank, you just told him that same shit ten minutes ago." Mack said cutting Tank off.

"Damn, I did?"

"Yeah, and I already did that shit." Rob spoke up. He was starting to feel the same way that Mack was feeling.

"You let them know that we gone park a block away from dude shit and march over there right?"

"Yeah, all that shit." Rob said as Mack pulled off after the light turned green.

☙

Steve, A.P. and the four riders that were with them, pulled up on 148th street and parked just down the block from Lil J's buildings. They were so charged up and ready to kill something that they weren't paying attention to their surroundings. They were under the impression that shit was sweet and that they wouldn't have to worry about anything until they made it to the buildings.

So as they were hopping out of their cars, cocking their guns, and getting ready to march down the block to meet Tank and the rest of their guys, they didn't see the two figures step out of the cut.

☙

Detective Bradly and Jones were eight blocks away from the Vail apartment parked on Lincoln. They were talking to one of their neighborhood snitches trying to find out the latest until they heard the shots ringing out in the distance.

"Hurry up and get out man, we gotta go." Detective Bradly said as he pulled off before their snitch was able to get his whole body out of the car.

☙

Chop! Chop! Chop! Chop! Was all that could be heard as J. J and Ant started letting their choppers ride. They had watched the two cars pull up and park on a street that nobody usually parked on, and once they saw that the guys getting out of the care were packing steel, they stepped out of the cut and gave it to their ass.

"A.P get up!" Steve hollered. Him and three of the riders had managed to get out of the line of fire without catching a bullet. A.P and the other rider weren't so fortunate; they caught the first few slugs from J. J's chopper and was laying on the curb leaking.

"A.P get up!" Steve hollered again.

"Man that nigga gone!" One of the riders hollered to Steve before he raised his Tech up over the car that he was hiding behind and let off a few wild shots that made J. J and Ant duck for cover.

When Steve snapped out of his trance and looked up the street, he saw two more gunners coming down the block. "What the fuck!" he hollered as he raised his chopper and let it spit in their direction.

CHAPTER 22

Lil J's building was two blocks away from the light on Dixie Highway, but Mack parked on the third block by the back parking lot.

"Ya'll ready?" Tank asked, after him and the rest of his guys got out of their cars.

"We was ready last week." His guys retorted.

"Aight then, let's go through here and shut this bitch down." Tank said as he cocked his chrome AK-47 before him, Mack, Rob, Red, Lil Bill, Tiny and the rest of the riders that were with them started creeping through the parking lot towards the back of the building.

When they heard gun shots coming from the next block they immediately thought it was Steve and A. P and started running only to be caught off guard by a rain of gun fire.

"OH SHIT!" Lil Bill hollered as a slug grazed his arm before he was able to dive behind a car.

Rob, Tiny and two of their riders were slaughtered. Tank, Mack, Red, and the last two riders managed to escape the rain.

"I knew this was a bad idea." Mack said as he started firing wild shots from the side of the car that he dove behind.

"Man shut yo bitch ass up and keep shooting!" Tank hollered back. He realized that it was a bad idea too, but it wasn't any turning back now. He had lost too many guys and was determined to end the war once and for all or at least take out Lil J.

෴

Lil J, Lunitic and Lunitic's guys had peeped Tank and his guys creeping through the parking lot and were planning on letting them get just a little bit closer before they opened fire, but once one of Lunitic's guys heard the gun shots from the other block and saw Tank and his guys running, he said fuck waiting, and raised his chopper and started blasting.

"Fuck." Lil J said to hisself as he started firing his AR-15. He wanted to make sure that he changed Tank when they opened fire, but it wasn't looking good now because he had watched him slide behind a car once Lunitic's guys started shooting. "Fuck this shit. Tic, cover me." Lil J said as he dipped low and started creeping.

"I ain't go'n." Lunitic said as he followed Lil J. "My guys can cover us."

ಬ

Man, this shit ain't looking good, Tank thought as he continued firing his AK. All of the gun shots were starting to wake him up and make him see a little clearer. He was on foreign land and didn't have enough troops. And the ones that he did have were decreasing in numbers. *Man this shit fucked up.*

"Tank, we gotta – " was as far as Mack got before Lil J and Lunitic stepped from around the car that he was behind and started fanning him and another one of the riders out, chopping their bodies to pieces.

"Fuck!" Tank said as he turned his AK in their direction and spit the last few shells before he pulled out his .44s "Red, you and Bill come on, it's ugly." He said as they continued to let their guns ride while crawfishing out of the parking lot at the same time.

ಬ

Lil J and Lunitic had dipped back on the other side of the car.

"I'm cool man, just go get that nigga." Lunitic said as Lil J tried to help him up off the ground. He had caught a slug in his thigh when Tank turned his AK in their direction.

"Fuck that nigga. We gotta get the fuck outta here before the police come."

"Aight, fuck him then." Lunitic said allowing Lil J to help him up. He had flashbacks of the county jail once Lil J brought up the police, and he damn sure wasn't trying to go back.

Zed was still posted in front of the buildings with his AR-15. He had sent Mal and B down to 148th to assist J. J and Ant. He could see the parking lot and 148th from where he was posted and wanted to go get a piece of the action, but knew that he couldn't because he had to watch the front and make sure that nobody tried to creep up on them. "What it is J?" he asked as he saw Lil J coming his way practically dragging Lunitic.

"Go get the car. We gotta get outta here."

"Where Zep and K.B at?"

"I don't know, but hurry up and get the car before the police come."

☙

"Ay Zep, check these mu'fuckas out in this car down the street." K.B said referring to a car that he watched pull up like three minutes ago. Him and Zep had pulled up and parked behind Tank and his guys after they watched them get out of their cars and walk towards the parking lot. They had planned on creeping up and catching them off guard, but once they heard the gun shots, they disregarded it because they didn't want to catch a bullet from their own guys.

But now that some of the shooting was subsiding, they dipped low behind their car and got on point in case Tank or some of his guys made it through the storm and tried to make it back to their cars.

"What about 'em?" Zep responded glancing down the street at the car.

"They pulled up a few minutes ago and still ain't got out the car yet."

"You think - ." Zep started but stopped as he saw Tank and three of his guys hustling out of the parking lot. "Fuck them, let's get these niggas." he said as he came from behind the car letting his chopper ride catching Lil Bill and Red.

Ain't this a bitch, Tank thought before he raised his .44s and threw some shells back. The first few slugs hit Zep in the chest and knocked him off his feet.

Chop! Chop! Chop! Chop! Was the sound of K. B's chopper as he ran amuck ending Tank and the last rider's career before they got to do any more damage. "What's up bruh? You cool?" he asked after he turned around and saw Zep getting up off the ground holding his chest.

"Drop your fucking weapons, this shit is over with!" Detective Bradly hollered as him and Detective Jones were walking up with their guns at the ready. They had watched everything go down and was now ready to take down the survivors.

"This some bitch ass shit." K. B said looking over his shoulder at the Detectives. "Zep, get the car ready. I'ma 'bout to burn these bitches." He said.

Boom! Boom! Boom!

Detective Bradly and Jones started firing. They hit K.B once in the side of his head, and four times in his back before he was able to turn his whole body around.

"Ahhhhh!" Zep hollered as he waved his chopper and pulled the trigger. Detective Bradly died instantly from the first few slugs and Detective Jones was critically injured by the rest. "K. Bbbbb!" he hollered, walking up on K. B's lifeless body. "K.B. get – " was as far as he got before he saw the blood coming from K.B's head. "Damn K.B……fuck." His eyes started tearing up. When he heard the sirens getting louder and saw the red and blue lights in the distance, he ran to his car and pulled off.

☙

"Just get me to my car and I'll be cool." said Lunitic.

"What about yo leg?" Lil J asked.

"I'll worry about that shit when me and my guys get back to – " Lunitic paused as he heard shots coming from the next block. "Damn, whoever that is getting it crack'n" he said after Zed pulled up with the car.

"That might be my Lil brother and K. B." said Zed.

"It might be, but we gotta get the fuck outta here." said Lil J.

☙

When Zed and Lil J pulled up to their building on 159th in Lexington, Zed chirped T.Y and told him to set-up some security before him and Lil J dipped into the cut.

"What the fuck happened back there?" Zed inquired.

"Tank and his guys tried to creep up on us and we fired they ass up."

"Did ya'll get Tank bitch ass?"

"Hell nah, but we got that nigga that changed Mikey."

"That's good shit." Zed said before his phone started going off. "What up?" he answered after looking at the caller I.D, and seeing that it was Zep.

"Where ya'll at?" Zep inquired.

"We on the nine."

"Man jo, K.B. dead!"

"What?"

"K. B – gone."

"What you mean he gone? What the fuck happened?"

"I'm on my way man. I'ma tell you when I get there."

"Aight." Zed said before he ended the call. "That was Zep." he said before he paused and shook his head. "He say we lost K. B."

He say we lost K.B. Lil J thought as he replayed Zed's words over in his head. He felt the same resentment that he felt when they lost Mikey. All of this was his fault, and his guys were paying for it. "What the fuck Zep say happened?"

"He didn't say, but he should be here in like five minutes."

"This shit fucked up man, we gotta get outta here. I'ma 'bout to run to one of my safe houses and pick up some paper. When Zep get here ya'll go do what ya'll gotta do, then meet me on Torrence by the E-way."

"Bet, but if you get there before us just wait at the White Castle." Zed said as him and Lil J embraced before Lil J went and jumped into one of the trap cars that they kept on the block and pulled off.

Two minutes later, Zep pulled up and hopped out of his whip.

Zed emerged from the cut. "Come on Lil bruh we gotta go pick up some paper real quick." he said as him and Zep jumped into one of the other trap cars and pulled off.

"Where Lil J at?" Zep inquired.

"You just missed him. He pulled off like three minutes before you pulled up." He went to pick up some money, but he gone meet us at the White Castle on Torrence."

"What we meeting on Torrence for?"

"That's where we gone get on the E-way at. What happened to K.B tho'?"

"Man, them bitches got down on him!" Zep said feeling the pain all over again. "I took care of them bitches for him tho'."

"Who got down on him? Who you talking about? Tank and them?"

"Nah, we took care of Tank, but right after we laid they ass down, Detective Bradly and Jones walked up and got down on K.B, but I took care of they ass tho'."

"You got down on the police?" Zed asked not believing what he had just heard.

"Hell yeah, I got down on 'em."

"We gotta hurry up and get the fuck outta here because the police about to be hot as hell." Zed said as they pulled up to their safe house.

☙

When Lil J made it to his safe house, he grabbed two hundred thousand dollars before he went and jumped back into his whip and pulled off. He was supposed to head to the White Castle on Torrence to meet Zed and Zep, but decided to turn his car around and head out to Thornton first because he wanted to see his son and drop some money off with his baby mama.

While he was on his way out to Thornton, he got a phone call from his cousin Greg. "What up cuz?" he answered.

"What's up man? I know you ain't still at the hospital."

"Nah, I been left from up there."

"What's up then? You gone meet me somewhere so we can holler?"

"I don't know man, it's a lot of shit going on in my hood, so I'ma 'bout to dip back outta town."

"Come on Lil cuz. I need to rotate with you about some real shit." said Greg. He was becoming very avid and persistent. "We can meet where ever cuz. I ain't gone hold you up that long."

'Aight man, I'm on my way out to Thornton right now, but you can meet me in River Oaks in thirty minutes." Lil J said before ending the call.

When he made it to Karina's house, he walked in and gave her fifty thousand. "Here bay, this a lil change for you and my son. I gotta disappear for awhile, but I'll be back soon." He said before he kissed her on the forehead.

"John, I haven't saw you in a whole week, and you already talking about disappearing again. When are you going to spend some time with me?"

"KL baby, I ain't got time for this shit right now. Some bullshit just came up and I gotta leave asap." Lil J said before he walked into his son's room and found him sound asleep.

Karina was right on Lil J's heels. "John, can you stay with me tonight and leave tomorrow?"

"Nah bay, it's a must that I leave asap. I got mu'fuka's waiting on me right now anyway." Lil J said as he bent down and kissed his son on the forehead before walking out of the room and heading towards the door.

Karina wasn't giving up. She was too determined. So she ran to the door and locked it before she took off her robe and exposed her beautiful body. "At least make love to me before you leave."

Damn, why the fuck did she do that? Lil J thought as he became aroused. *Zed and Zep gon' be mad as hell at me, but fuck it.* "Yo freaky ass don't give up do you?" he asked as he began taking off his shirt and vest.

"Nope." Karina said with a big smile on her face.

"I love you too much to give up." she said as she walked over and helped him take off the rest of his clothes before throwing her tongue into his mouth.

They kissed hungrily for about twenty seconds before Lil J picked Karina up and pinned her to the wall before sliding inside of her.

"Bay, promise me that you gone let me go after this." Lil J said as he began thrusting in and out of her.

"Unnh…bay I … Unnh… I don't… Unnh… I don't' wanna let you… Unnh." Karina moaned.

"Bay… promise me." Lil J said again before he began thrusting harder.

"OH bay… Unnnh…..baay."

"Promise me." he said as he picked up the pace.

"OOH…Unnh…I…Unnh..I promise… Ooh I promise..Unnh..bay… I'm… I'm cum'n..baaayyy." Karina exclaimed as she came hard.

Lil J still hadn't cum yet, so he continued to thrust until he exploded all inside of her.

"Bay, I love you." Karina said after she laid her head on Lil J's shoulder.

"I love you too." Lil J said as he pulled out of Karina before lowering her to the floor.

Karina still had her arms wrapped around Lil J's neck, and didn't want to let go.

When Lil J heard his phone ring, he immediately thought about Zed and Zep. "Bay, I gotta go."

"I don't want you to." Karina said as she began crying.

"Bay, please don't start this shit. You promised me that you was gone let me go."

"Okay, I'm sorry, just promise me that you gone come back." she said as she allowed Lil J to unwrap her arms from around his neck.

"I promise bay." Lil J said before he went and put his clothes back on. He left his vest on the floor and told Karina to put it up for him before he left out of the house.

CHAPTER 23

The White Castle on Torrence was known as a live spot at night, where a lot of ballers went to stunt and floss their whips, so when Zed and Zep pulled up in their trap car and parked in the cut, they went unnoticed.

The bitches were up there half naked shaking their asses, while the niggas stood next to their cars with their suicide doors up letting their music blast.

"Lil J need to hurry up man. I'm tired of looking at all of these fake ass wanna be ballers. I remember when me and K.B used to come through here and shut this bitch down. Him in his Pepsi colored Chevy with the pelle leather guts sitting on eights, and me in my cayenne and red L. S. Monte Carlo with the peanut butter rag and the peanut butter guts."

"The one with the sixes on it?" Zed asked helping his little brother vibe.

"Yeah." Zep replied as his eyes began to tear up. He looked at K.B like the baby brother that he never had. He loved him to death and would do anything to bring him back.

Zed saw his brother's eyes water up and changed the subject because he didn't want to see him cry. "We been up here for over three and a half hours and this nigga still ain't showed up or returned our calls. I wonder where the fuck he at."

"You think the police got him?"

"Shit, its' either that or his ass done stopped over a bitch crib."

"Call his phone again."

Zed grabbed his phone and dialed a few numbers before putting it to his ear. After about six rings, Lil J's phone went to voicemail. "He still ain't answering."

"That nigga probably locked up, but I hope he somewhere fucking a bitch."

"He was just telling me how he was falling for Beautyful too. I hope he ain't try'da go pick her up on some dumb shit."

"You got that bitch number?"

"Hell nah, but I can call one of the shorties in the crack spot on the block and have somebody go check to see if he came through." Zed said before he dialed the crack spot. "Damn."

"What?"

"The mu'fucka went straight to voicemail."

"Don't you got that bitch Bianca number?" Zep asked, already knowing that his brother had the number. "Call that hoe and get Beautyful number."

"Right." Zed said before dialing Bianca's number. She answered on the fourth ring.

"What's up Zed? What the hell going on over there at ya'll buildings?"

"What you mean?"

"The police all through that mu'tha fucka. I just got off the phone with my cousin and she – "

"Where the fuck she at?"

"She at the buildings getting harassed by the police."

"Right now?"

"Yeah, she say –"

"I'ma hit you back." Zed said before he hung up. He knew that Lil J couldn't have been fucking with Beautyful if she was still at the buildings. "The bitch say the police all over the block."

"What about Beautyful?"

"She say Beautyful over there getting harassed by the police right now."

"Fuck could this nigga be?" Zep fumed.

"I don't know, but we ain't about to keep sitting up here."

"Call his B.M crib. If he ain't there, then he gotta be locked up."

After Zed dialed Karina's number, the phone rang three times before a baby's voice came through the line.

"Hello."

"Lil Malik."

"Huh?"

"What's up man? This yo Uncle Zed."

"Hey Uncle Zed. My Mommy crying."

"What's wrong? Why she crying?"

"She cry cause Daddy gone."

I knew this nigga was with a bitch. He probably told her that he was leaving town and she got mad and didn't want him to leave. But lil Malik said he was gone so he should be on his way. "Lil Malik."

"Huh?"

"I'ma talk to you la - ."

"Hello. Hello." Karina sobbed into the phone.

"How you doing Karina?" Zed asked feeling out of character.

This was his man B.M and he didn't feel like going through the complications with her, knowing that her and Lil J probably just got through arguing.

"Who is this?" Karina asked sounding terrible.

"Zed."

"Ohhh Zeedd." she sobbed harder. "They got himmm. Hee gonnee."

"What? Who got him? What you mean he gone?" Zed inquired flummoxed.

"He gone! Who gone? What she talking about?" Zep asked fearing the worst.

Zed ignored Zep and tried to decipher what Karina was saying.

"Heee gonne Zeedd. Theyy shot him uup!"

"What? When? Who shot him up?" Zed asked wishing that he had heard wrong but knowing that he didn't.

"Who got shot up Zed? Who gone? What she talking about?"

"Man hold the fuck on!" Zed said fumingly, not really meaning to snap the way that he did.

"I don't know. He left out of the house and then I heard gun shots." Karina said trying to control herself. "After the gun shots stopped, I went to the window and saw him on the ground trying to get up, so I went out there to help him and —" was as far as she got before she went back to crying uncontrollably.

"It's gone be okay Karina, just calm down." Zed lied.

He knew that things wouldn't be okay, and he was beginning to feel bad for making her relive the loss of her son's father. "I'm on my way over there." he said before hanging up. He needed to find out what else she knew. Something had to come up.

Lil J's murder wouldn't go unanswered. Tank and most of his guys were dead, so it couldn't have been them unless somebody from his crew made it through the storm and followed them.

He needed to find out if the money that Lil J picked up was gone. Maybe somebody followed him from his safe house and tried to rob him. Whatever it was, he vowed to soon find out and then venge Lil J's death.

When Zed pulled up to Karina's block, he saw that two squad cars were parked in front of her crib so he kept it moving. He didn't want to get harassed, questioned or locked up, so he called Karina and told her that he would be to see her after things cooled down before him and Zep went and hopped on the E-way and left town.

CHAPTER 24

Out in the Bahamas, Rick was laid back on the beach soaking up the sun while two Jamaican cuties were catering to him.

"Kadean." Rick called out after his phone started ringing.

"Wha'pen?" Kadean replied.

"Grab my phone outta that bag for me." Rick said as he prepared hisself to hear some bad news before Kadean handed him his phone. "Speak." he said after looking at the caller I. D.

"Our friends cured the disease."

"Are you sure?"

"Positive."

A smile spread across Rick's face. "I'll be home in a week." He said, before ending the call.

To Be Continued…